D0977444

Viviane

Viviane

Julia Deck

Translated by Linda Coverdale

THE NEW PRESS

NEW YORK
LONDON

The New Press gratefully acknowledges the Florence Gould
Foundation for supporting publication of this book.

Copyright © 2012 by Les Éditions de Minuit,
7, rue Bernard-Palissy, 75006 Paris
English translation copyright © 2014 by The New Press
All rights reserved.
No part of this book may be reproduced, in any form,
without written permission from the publisher.

Requests for permission to reproduce selections from
this book should be mailed to: Permissions Department,
The New Press, 120 Wall Street, 31st floor, New York, NY 10005.

Originally published in France as *Viviane Élisabeth
Fauville* by Les Éditions de Minuit, Paris, 2012
Published in the United States by The New Press, New York, 2014
Distributed by Perseus Distribution

LIBRARY OF CONGRESS CATALOGING-IN-PUBLICATION DATA

Deck, Julia.
[Viviane Élisabeth Fauville. English]
Viviane : a novel / By Julia Deck ; Translated by Linda Coverdale.
pages cm
Originally published in France as Viviane Élisabeth Fauville by
Les Editions de Minuit, Paris, 2012.
ISBN 978-1-59558-964-4 (hardback)—
ISBN 978-1-59558-971-2 (e-book)
1. Families—Fiction. I. Title.
PQ2704.E248V5813 2012
843'.92—dc23   2013039843

The New Press publishes books that promote and enrich public
discussion and understanding of the issues vital to our democracy
and to a more equitable world. These books are made possible by
the enthusiasm of our readers; the support of a committed group of
donors, large and small; the collaboration of our many partners in the
independent media and the not-for-profit sector; booksellers, who often
hand-sell New Press books; librarians; and above all by our authors.

www.thenewpress.com

Composition by dix!
This book was set in Stempel Garamond

Printed in the United States of America

2   4   6   8   10   9   7   5   3   1

I have been here, ever since I began to be,
my appearances elsewhere
having been put in by other parties.

—Samuel Beckett, *The Unnamable*

Viviane

I

The child is twelve weeks old, and her breathing lulls
you with the calm, even rhythm of a metronome. The
two of you are sitting in a rocking chair in the middle
of an essentially empty room. The boxes stacked up by
the movers line the wall on the right. Three of them,
at the top of the pile, have been opened to obtain the
most urgently needed items: kitchen utensils, toiletries,
some clothing, and the baby's things, which outnumber
yours. The window has no curtain. It seems tacked onto
the wall like a sketch, a pure study in perspective, in
which the railway tracks and overhead wires streaking
away from the Gare de l'Est would provide the vanish-
ing lines.

You are not entirely sure, but it seems to you that
four or five hours ago, you did something that you
shouldn't have. You try to recall what you did, to

reconstruct the sequence of your actions, but whenever you remember something, instead of automatically calling the next action to mind, it stumbles into the hole your memory has become.

Actually, you aren't even certain that you returned a little while ago to that other apartment you've been visiting secretly for years. The contours, the masses, the colors and décor all meld in the distance. That man who received you there, did he even exist? And anyway, if you had done something wrong, you would not be sitting idly here. You would be going around in circles, chewing your nails to the quick, so guilt-ridden you couldn't see anything straight. On the contrary, you're perfectly calm: in spite of your hazy memory, you feel quite free and easy.

Your hips stop moving, no longer rocking the chair. You carry the baby into the next room. This one is somewhat more furnished. Flanking the window are a cradle and a single bed, the coverlet smoothly taut, the top sheet folded over it. The child hardly fusses at all and falls asleep again when you lay her down on her back. You glance around, straighten the heaps of clothes partly concealing a wooden chest under the window, run your hand down the dress at the front of a rolling metal clothes rack holding all your winter coats and pants. The sweaters are stacked on the shelf above; the boots and shoes sit patiently in pairs between the casters.

A hall links the two rooms and the kitchen. At the end is the bathroom, a tiny nook where, sitting on the toilet, you find your knees bumping the sink and your left foot wedged against the edge of the shower stall. Strips of paint are peeling slowly from the ceiling. The place should have been spruced up but you wanted to take possession as soon as possible and told the landlord you'd take care of that yourself after moving in, he need only forgive you a month's rent. As for the kitchen, no complaints there. The latest built-in appliances beneath a countertop of faux granite, gleaming plumbing, and the sparkling tile floor are enough to justify the exorbitant rent.

You take two eggs from the fridge and a bowl from the cupboard over the sink to whip up an omelet. Most people believe an omelet should be smooth in texture, and most people are mistaken. The artistry lies in just barely introducing the white to the yolk, then cooking them only until they seize up. You have often watched your mother beating eggs for an omelet. Her instructions are engraved in your memory, and this pretty much sums up your talents in the way of domestic accomplishments. You are well educated, have a fine professional career. Such activities leave little time for becoming the perfect housewife. Which you regret, for in your bleakest hours, you'll listen to the first person who comes along, and there are still people who claim that perfect housewifery is the way to hold on to a husband.

While you're whisking the eggs with a fork, you try to remember what you did today. The baby woke you up at six o'clock: a faint whimper arises in the bedroom, still dark despite the absence of shutters. You open one eye, murmur a silly tune, one of those pop songs learned at fifteen, the only lullabies you know. Then you set the bottle to warm and slip into the shower in the meantime. The child winds up in your arms in the kitchen, she has her bottle, and both your minds go blank. Then you park her back in the cradle for a few minutes while you get her things together, brush your hair, apply some eyeliner. Together you go outside.

The babysitter lives on Rue Chaudron. From your building, on the corner of Rue Cail and Rue Louis-Blanc, it's straight ahead then left then right. The sitter provides the minimum of service. She keeps the place scrupulously clean, surrounds the child with impeccable care, and never bothers with useless courtesies. This suits you to a T. You'll be going back to work in a month, and the little girl should get a tad used to doing without you.

Until two in the afternoon, you're busy with administrative formalities concerning the move to the new apartment, the divorce, and single-parent benefits. You also buy a few clothes and go to the hairdresser, where you agree to a manicure. Once upon a time, your friends who were already mothers liked to say that you were so lucky to have time to tend to yourself. You resolved, should your luck ever change, to spare your offspring any responsibility for tarnished maternal beauty.

The omelet is now just right. You fold it into a half moon with the spatula and slide it onto a plastic plate, tapping the edge to hear the sound of this bizarre substance that mimics china so well. You bought it at the Monoprix department store in the Gare du Nord. Without paying close attention, as you were too busy studying another customer out of the corner of your eye. He was about your age, examining the same items. You would have liked to know if he, too, was in emergency mode, forced to leave behind the family dishes, but you didn't dare ask.

Over the center of the half moon, you pour the
contents of a can of peas and carrots and put the whole
thing into the microwave, a slight twist on the art of the
omelet, while you return to what you did this morning.
It does appear that you did in fact go to your husband's
apartment: you still have the key, and you'd wanted to
pick up a few items.

The apartment on Rue Louis-Braille hasn't changed
over the past month. Julien says he's going to move
out but it's dragging on. In any case, he doesn't seem
to spend much time here. The sink and dish rack are
empty, there's no plastic bag in the garbage pail, and the
TV magazine dates from before you left. You claim a
square platter, a few bath towels, and the toaster. While
you're hunting in the closet of the second bedroom—the
one intended for the baby—for a carryall to transport
everything, you come across your wedding presents.
Now, there is no reason why this man who loved you
so little, whom you desired so much, and who disappointed you so deeply should keep a set of eight kitchen
knives given by your mother on that special occasion.
You carried off the knives in your purse, and it's not too
bad at all to have remembered that. You finish the last
mouthful of omelet and go to bed.

2

The next morning, Tuesday, November 16, your memory has completely returned. The digital clock down by the foot of the bed says 5:03. There's about an hour left before the child wakes up, one hour in which to find a solution, to clear away as much as possible of the debris strewn all around you.

You are Viviane Élisabeth Fauville, wife of Julien Hermant. You are forty-two years old and on August 23 you gave birth to your first child, who will no doubt remain your only one. You are the public relations officer for the Biron Concrete Company. This business earns lots of money and is headquartered in an eight-story building on Rue de Ponthieu, two steps from the Champs-Élysées. In the reception area, willowy women entertain visitors with slightly racy small talk.

Your husband, Julien Antoine Hermant, a civil

engineer in the Highways Department, was born forty-three years ago in the small provincial town of Nevers. On September 30 he put an end to two years of conjugal misery. He said Viviane—coming home at some late hour from his so-called planning department—Viviane I'm leaving, it's the only solution, anyway you know that I'm cheating on you and that it isn't even from love but from despair.

You absorbed this rib-crushing blow with perfect impassibility. Your shoulders barely shrugged, the rhythm of the rocking chair barely faltered, your fingers barely tightened on the armrests. Viviane he said again, listen to me, you have the child whereas I—I need some air. And I can't give you what you want, maybe you expect too much from me. Viviane, I'm begging you, say something.

You said no, I'm the one who's leaving. Keep everything, I'm taking the child, we won't need alimony. You moved out on October 15, found a babysitter, extended your maternal leave for health reasons, and on Monday, November 15—yesterday—you killed your psychoanalyst. You did not kill him symbolically, the way one sometimes ends up killing the father. You killed him with a Zwilling J.A. Henckels Twin Profection santoku knife. "The unique forging of the blade's edge offers optimal stability and exceptional ease in cutting," explained the brochure you were studying at Galeries Lafayette while your mother was getting out her checkbook.

This knife, which belongs to a set of eight, you picked up at Julien's apartment sometime that morning. You grabbed the case without a moment's hesitation. It went straight to the bottom of your purse, the zipper of which you closed with a firm yank. Then something very strange happened. You were about to leave the apartment; your hand had already grasped the doorknob when a black veil fell over the room. Suddenly you were no longer leaving the apartment, it was the apartment that was swirling around you, rising on all sides, floor, walls, ceiling, as everything was suddenly overturned. Sweat pearled in the palms of your hands as thousands of insects thrummed inside your skull, a swarming army attacking the slightest bits of bare skin, blocking exits, closing off your eyes, nose, and mouth.

You slumped down on the linoleum, your head on your knees to help blood reach the brain. Dug the bottle of mineral water out of your purse. Drank a few swallows, prayed to God knows whom, hoping that the terror would fade away. From beneath a low cabinet, the cat's yellow eyes—all that was visible in the darkness—observed you cautiously.

At last you remembered that you regularly consult a specialist. When your fingers stopped trembling so much, you grabbed your cell phone, scrolled through your address book, and selected Shrink.

He answered in his usual offhand tone because he was with a patient and because that is his normal voice. The doctor doesn't bother with formalities, they are against his code of ethics and detrimental to the cure, as he has told you many times. You're already lucky that he has agreed to see you in this emergency, at six thirty tonight, a canceled appointment. In any case, he's been nagging you for months to move up to three sessions a week.

You went home to drop off the carryall with the toaster, then on to the sitter's to ask her if, this once, she would keep the baby until that evening. But no, she does not find that convenient at all. You take your daughter home, nurse her, and spend the afternoon in the rocking chair searching for a solution.

Actually, you have already found one, you're simply trying to get used to the idea. Whenever the baby falls asleep, she's out for three hours. This will leave plenty of time to dash off to the 5th arrondissement, a direct shot on the 7 line. You will shut off the gas, unplug the heating unit, and you will not lock the apartment door so that the firemen can get in easily if a fire breaks out in spite of all your precautions. Such arrangements clearly cast no luster on your maternal instincts. You're not proud of this and will not be gaily recounting the scene to your eight- or nine-year-old daughter when she decides to start finding fault with you, having established by comparison with the classics of children's literature that you are not the ideal mother glorified by family-values novels. So there it is, you won't tell a soul, ever: you know how to keep your little secrets.

Toward the end of the afternoon, you feed the child, put her to bed, then head up Rue de l'Aqueduc to the métro station. Censier-Daubenton is seventeen stops and a good half hour away. By the time you arrive, night has almost fallen. In two minutes you have crossed the square and reached Rue de la Clef, which is deserted. You do not meet anyone while going up to the fourth floor of No. 22A, either. You ring and, when the buzzer sounds, you enter the waiting room. Five minutes later there's a murmured au revoir, followed by the closing of the landing door. You're kept waiting while someone apparently makes a few phone calls, has a smoke at the window. You leaf idly through the only reading material within reach, a boring seventeenth-century play by Pierre Corneille. The fan of pages is coming loose from the binding. No real effort seems to have been made to alleviate the stage fright of those waiting for the curtain to go up, and now you think, in hindsight, that if there'd been a *Paris Match* or any other magazine available, something even vaguely intended to relieve your distress instead of reinforce it, you might not have wound up where you are.

The doctor receives you after a long fifteen minutes, wearing a small satisfied smile. Stepping back to let you pass, he even seems to bow slightly.

So, he begins, with false good humor, as if he were about to tell you a good story. But this is a trick, an infallible way to make the patient fall into the trap. You've been aware of this trick for a long time yet cannot resist the doctor's mysterious power.

It reappeared this morning, you begin. It had gone away while I was pregnant, now it's back. I wound up on the floor in my place, well really in my husband's place, in what used to be my apartment. Something needs to be done, I can't take it anymore, I have to look after my daughter.

The doctor says yes.

Yes what? you reply. I'm telling you something must be done, no yes or no about it. I haven't come here to go all the way back to the Flood, I'm tired, I need help now.

But you know perfectly well, Madame Fauville, excuse me, Hermant, you know that the symptoms are only symptoms. That one must go back to their source, isn't that so, Madame Hermant?

My dear doctor, I tell you I couldn't care less about their source. For three years now you've been running me around in circles, three years of the same old same old. If you can't do anything for me, just say so, I'll go somewhere else.

Yes?

Doctor, you're not listening to me. I don't want to play anymore, I give up. Some other method is required or there's no point in my coming here again.

Really now, blackmail.

This has nothing to do with blackmail, you announce, raising your voice just a little. On the contrary. I would like to stay, I would like this to work, but I can't go on endlessly with no results. I haven't the means.

The means?

Yes, the means, right, the means, and now you're yelling. The time, the money, the necessary resources. There are the bills, the rent, the babysitter, it's not my husband who's going to help me out here, must I remind you, my husband who left me for some fresh young idiot or other, so I'm on my own, as the saying goes, on my own with my daughter, we're two on-our-owns and we need to get out of this mess.

Why have you made this choice?

You clench your fists, squash your spine against the back of the armchair and close your eyes. A tiny rain of rage escapes from the corners of your eyelids. You see yourself again, a month and a half earlier, hunched deep in the rocking chair in the Rue Louis-Braille apartment, facing your husband as he dismisses you, trying to keep calm by deciding on the spot to move out because it was your last chance to take him by surprise.

You snatch up your purse. Fumbling for some tissues, you feel the case of knives, which is rather heavy, but you were in such a hurry when you left your place, so uneasy at the idea of leaving your daughter alone, that you'd paid no attention to it. You find the tissues; the purse sits open on your lap.

I didn't choose anything, it's my husband who left me.

But we all make unconscious choices.

You're suggesting that I pushed him out.

I'm not suggesting anything, you're the one who's saying that.

Your arms jerk up from the armrests and your hands begin to shake.

Listen, Madame Hermant, here's what we'll do. You'll take these pills for me for a few months, you know, the antidepressants, plus the ones for when your nerves give way, they'll help stabilize the hysteria. They worked rather well the last time, didn't they, Madame Hermant? Here, I'm writing you a prescription. Be nice now, start the treatment again, come back to see me on Wednesday, and we'll move to three sessions a week. Monday at eight, does that suit you?

Suddenly you are quite calm again. The doctor has found just the right word. Nice. You will never be that again. Your fingers rummage in the purse, find their way into the knife box, feel the blades and remove the largest knife from the ring securing it to the synthetic velvet lining. You take the knife out of the purse, stand up, step forward. The doctor is still smiling, waiting for what happens next as if he were at the theater. Naturally he doesn't believe you're capable of this, either. He has never seen you as anything but a colorless middle-class careerist, a run-of-the-mill neurotic to be brought to heel with blue or white pills. At last he will see what you're made of. And in fact, as you close in, the sneering laughter dies down while his flabby features freeze. But when he realizes what's coming, it's way too late.

You're only inches away, towering over him with your height and high heels. You raise the knifepoint to his stomach, clumsily, as if feeling your way, not quite sure if this will work. He opens his mouth wide; a cry gathers deep in his throat. Then you know you must not hesitate: you shove the knife in just below the lowest rib, up to the hilt. The viscera are as soft as butter. You move up toward the lung but already the little man is expiring, lying prostrate before the armchair from which he will no longer play the tyrant with anyone.

The bloodstain seeps into the blue shirt. Soon it's a puddle on his left side, then a pool spreading to the rug. You move the toes of your shoes out of the way. You have nothing in mind, no strategy, but perhaps some memory of a film or crime novel prompts you to consider that it might be better not to be seen, in the next few minutes, leaving the doctor's office looking haggard and splotched with blood. You wipe the knife on your pullover; the liquid soaks through the wool to wet the skin of your abdomen. In the pocket of your raincoat you find a plastic bag scrunched into a ball. The knife gets wrapped in that. You check to make sure you haven't forgotten anything, leave the room and at least a thousand pieces of evidence behind but, overwhelmed, you couldn't find them even if you stayed all night, having never thought of polishing up your skills as a murderess.

Rue de la Clef is as empty as it was a little while ago. The first person you come across is a young woman at the corner of Rue Monge, with a baguette under one arm, a little boy hanging on the other, and a grumpy Monday-night expression. You reach the intersection where the métro station is, as well as several brasseries with heated terraces and therefore dozens of customers who have nothing better to do than watch the traffic and note the most picturesque passersby. You dive into the subway.

On the platform, the electronic display shows a three-minute wait for the next train. You sit down on an orange seat, stealthily examining the nearest travelers:

three young men in suits; two female students with studs in their noses, eyebrows, and the lobes of their pretty ears; an African man draped in an ample green native costume. You wait for them to unmask you. It must show in your face, that you just killed a man. And yet the African is absorbed in a free daily paper, the students are watching the mice scurrying around the tracks, and the others discuss the latest sales figures for the auto industry.

The train enters the station. The passengers press up against the windows until the doors open, pour out onto the platform, pour obediently back inside at the urging of the warning beeps, and the new arrivals elbow their way into the car. You move slowly into the heart of the crowd. A few men consider you absentmindedly, but your face seems to vanish from memory as soon as they look away.

At Stalingrad, the human surge throws you off the train and up to the surface, on Boulevard de la Cha-pelle. In five minutes you're outside your building. You don't see a single soul on your way up to the sixth floor, apart from the white cat on the third, who has finished his rounds and is waiting for someone to let him back into his apartment. Hunting for your keys in the outer pocket of your purse, you remember that you don't need them, you didn't lock the door. One twist of the doorknob and you hear the burbling coming from the cradle: the baby has only just awakened. You run to the washing machine to throw in all your clothes. Completely naked under the equally naked bulb, you clean the knife with dish detergent, bleach, and turpentine, then put it away with the others in its case. You warm the bottle; cradle the little girl; she feeds and falls asleep. Seated in the rocking chair in the middle of the bare living room, you forget.

3

The next morning, Tuesday, November 16, memory has completely returned. The digital clock down by the foot of the bed says 5:58. There are about two minutes left before the child wakes up, two minutes in which to find a solution, to clear away as much as possible of the debris strewn around by the previous day.

Viviane gets up and goes over to the cradle. With the tip of an index finger, she nudges the mobile attached to one edge by a curved metal stem. It's a little merry-go-round of lions and giraffes, the former suspended one notch above the latter, which therefore seem safely out of reach. But if you nudge the mobile a bit harder, the animals now not only turn around but dance up and down as well, which means anything can happen. The child opens one eye. Surprised to see her mother already there, she forgets to cry.

After leaving her with the sitter, Viviane heads straight for Boulevard de la Chapelle. She's wearing a houndstooth ensemble beneath her gray coat, the clouds are streaming away precisely parallel to the railway tracks, and everything seems very organized. She takes the 5 line in the métro, which drops her off six minutes later at République, where she switches to the 8 line bound for Créteil-Préfecture. It's obvious: the murder weapon must go back where she found it. Of course one can simply get rid of it in the Seine, but it's always when one goes to dispose of the incriminating evidence that a witness just happens to pop up, luckily for the law. Yes, the knife must go back to Julien's place, to the shelf where it has slept ever since it arrived, instead of resting quietly in a kitchen drawer from which one would remove it, once a week, to dissect the Sunday roast.

Emerging from the métro at Michel-Bizot, Viviane takes Rue de Toul to Louis-Braille. Number 35 is a middling-size apartment building constructed sometime during the 1970s. She crosses the small garden, pushes open the door, and runs into the concierge washing the floor beneath the mailboxes.

Ah, Madame Hermant, how nice. Imagine, I just saw your husband yesterday evening. With someone.

Don't worry, she's much too young for him. Be patient and he'll come back, believe me, and crawling, too.

Thank you, thanks, Viviane stammers in confusion. I was wondering if he'd left any mail in the box.

Um, no, I think he took it up. But I still have the key for upstairs. If you like, we can go take a look.

Viviane couldn't have asked for more, to be invited in without appearing to have her own key. She carefully avoids the damp area where the mop has passed while the concierge looks in her lodge for the keys and then follows her upstairs, where she opens the apartment door without a qualm, as if she spent every day snooping around empty premises. She peeks under both a cushion on the sofa and the TV schedule in the kitchen, then announces without further details, well I'm going to look around in the bedroom. Viviane hurries down the hall after her, then nips into the second bedroom. While the other woman inspects the master bedroom, Viviane puts the knife case back.

Aha, looky here, crows the concierge on the other side of the wall. Joining her, Viviane sees that she has picked up, at the foot of the bed, a scrap of shiny plastic that might well be a condom wrapper, but once the concierge has unfolded it, disappointment: the contents were simply chewing gum. Viviane shows her the old slippers snatched up from the back of the closet to justify having lingered in the other bedroom: I thought I'd pick these up as long as I'm here. Oh, go right ahead, dear, whyever would you leave that man any presents, after all. They finish touring the apartment; there is no mail anywhere. Viviane leaves the concierge to lock up. Thanks anyway, Madame Urdapilla, it was really nice to see you.

Then she walks to Place Félix-Éboué, where she orders a plain ham baguette sandwich and a sparkling water in a brasserie—no, give me a glass of wine instead, white, yes, that's fine. Outside the glass-enclosed terrace, the eight bronze lions of the fountain spit out water like lamas. Tiring of the lions, Viviane chews on a bite of sandwich, spots a copy of a daily paper lying on the end of the counter, and stops chewing.

Flipping through the front pages of *Le Parisien*, of no interest to her, she stops at page thirteen, which has news-in-brief items, then homes in on the lower left column headed "Homicide": "A secretary kills her ex-boyfriend." Nothing to be learned there. The thirty-nine-year-old woman was questioned three hours after the incident in her home in Normandy. Detectives know their job, they're specialists in this kind of amateur murderess. So what are the police doing? It's half past twelve. The doctor has been dead since yesterday evening and must have been found quickly—a patient, a worried wife stuck with the leg of lamb and parsley potatoes getting cold. There would have been weeping and wailing; a neighbor would have rushed to the scene of the crime and dialed the emergency number in front of the wild-eyed widow.

Sooner or later, the phone will ring: a detective would like to know how Viviane spent her evening, why she asked for an urgent appointment, because the patient who was there with the doctor that morning when he took the call will have reported their conversation. All they had to do was go through the doctor's address book to find out with whom he was speaking; you're so stupid, Viviane, really so stupid, you should have taken his phone, it was right there on the desk, you remember that perfectly.

Before folding up the paper, she consults the horoscope on the last page: "Love: Something is changing in your relationship. Success: You might find yourself at a kind of turning point. Health: A little nervous tension." She drains her glass and leaves the brasserie, considers taking the métro, then decides to proceed on foot. She walks and thinks faster and faster beneath the methodically aligned clouds overhead. With a bit of luck, the police will be swamped with work. And anyway, the success rate in homicides is what?—80 percent according to government statistics, not counting judicial errors, so that makes at least a 20 percent chance of going scot-free she thinks as she goes along Rue Faidherbe and Rue Saint-Maur. Besides, there is no criminal record or motive, and the doctor considered her such a boring patient that his files can't possibly contain anything suspicious. Viviane goes around the Hôpital Saint-Louis on its north-northwest side. About five hundred feet to the right and she's back at Place du Colonel-Fabien, and now it's a straight shot home, and now in the pocket of her big gray coat the phone begins to vibrate.

4

Set back from Place Maubert and hidden by a row of local shops, the police headquarters of the 5th arrondissement occupies a large city block bounded by Boulevard Saint-Germain, Rue de la Montagne-Sainte-Geneviève, Rue des Carmes, and Rue Basse-des-Carmes. Intentionally or not, its architecture seems to have been inspired by a military esthetic exemplified by the bunkers, blockhouses, and submarine bases built by the Germans along the French coasts during the Occupation. In short, it's pretty ugly.

Crossing the lobby, their clenched fists clammy with perspiration, Viviane and her daughter arouse no interest among the officers in confab around the security gate. The clerk at the information counter, however, studies this mother with a touch of suspicion upon learning that she has been summoned by Inspector

Philippot of the Criminal Investigation Division. Well of course she has no idea what he wants, shut up Viviane, you're getting confused, digging yourself in deeper, shut up. Go to the fourth floor, replies the clerk, and wait there until you're called.

Stepping out of the elevator, she sees plastic chairs lined up in front of offices with blue-tinted glazed partitions and Venetian blinds. It all looks exactly like the cop shows on television. Upon closer inspection, though, police housekeeping leaves much to be desired and the walls could use a lick of paint.

An officer signals to Viviane to sit down and she sits down. Watching the comings and goings in the corridor, she can easily tell the plainclothes police, moving casually around the offices, from the real civilians tiptoeing in or dashing for the exit. After fifteen minutes the baby begins to fuss, cry, and finally scream outrageously. Everyone looks at Viviane, who blushingly rises to pace the corridor. She whispers comforting words to her daughter but so unconvincingly, since she herself has little reason to feel reassured, that the child only wails even louder.

A door opens to reveal a very tall, very handsome man. He towers over the mother by a good head and slips a sidelong glance at the infant, who clams up. Come in, says Inspector Philippot, let's end this agony. They enter an office with a table piled high with files, a chair on either side, an old computer in a corner, and no charm whatsoever.

So, my dear lady, you are a patient of Dr. Jacques Sergent. How did you learn about his death? Then he stares piercingly at Viviane who has gone completely mindless. The policeman's head is perfectly smooth and he has full lips, like a pale-eyed Yul Brynner. His sky-blue shirt matches his eyes, his sandy jacket matches his skin. He's about fifty-three, fifty-four. She likes him a lot. She likes him a lot and he's going to nab her because he doesn't seem like an idiot.

He's dead? she asks innocently but without much hope. How could he be dead? I saw him the other day, he was fine, and who's going to take care of me now?

Funny, that's what they all say, notes the inspector ironically. When was your last appointment?

I was there Friday. Yes, Friday, I had a noon appointment. That's been my schedule for the last two months, with the Wednesday one at ten a.m. Before that I was pregnant, she explains, indicating her daughter with a tiny jut of her chin, the way one points to vegetables at the market or change lying on a counter.

And it went well?

I'm not going to lie to you, says Viviane after a pause during which she thinks I'd be better off lying, then no, I'm a lousy liar, he'll never believe me, and finally, let's be frank, maybe I can buy myself some credit. So Viviane says, I'm not going to lie to you, it never goes very well.

Yes?

Yes what? she shoots back. Sorry, he used to say that. He would keep saying yes instead of answering my questions, it was very irritating.

You're nervous.

Correct, I'm nervous, that's why I consult a specialist.

But he gets on your nerves.

So what are you trying to make me say, that I have problems? Because I can confess to that right now. Yes, I have plenty of problems and I'm worn out, my husband has left me, and she starts to cry.

Okay okay okay, the inspector says, because although he's relentless in his search for the truth, he doesn't seem too comfortable with personal secrets. And what were you doing last night between five and midnight?

I was home with my daughter, says Viviane, sniffling but without worrying because that's hardly a lie:

at five she was there, at home with her daughter, and at midnight as well. Then she adds too quickly, if you don't believe me, you can ask my mother. She called me around eight, she'll tell you, now excuse me, I'm going to take a tablet to calm down.

You're on medication?

The doctor had me take some now and then. But they're completely ordinary prescriptions, see, I've got one with me.

Yul glances at the paper, jots down a few words, probably the name of the drugs, and hands back the prescription. Viviane's stomach is heaving. It's the prescription the doctor wrote her yesterday, with the date in the upper right-hand corner. Her fingers are shaking as she puts it back in her purse, but Yul's mind is elsewhere. She doesn't seem to interest him very much and how can she resent him for that? She can tell that this interrogation makes her seem like a soon-to-be divorcée, garden variety, and such dry soil isn't fertile terrain for murderous germs and deadly herbs.

But tell me, dear lady, why did you call the doctor at ten thirty-eight yesterday morning?

Think fast, Viviane, think, say something, anything to break this guilty silence. Well, yes, she finally replies,

I was feeling faint. He gave me an emergency appointment at six thirty but I couldn't make it, I didn't find anyone to look after my daughter, just ask my mother.

And you couldn't have mentioned that earlier?

I thought, pleads Viviane as she begins crying again, that it would look suspicious even though you can see I had nothing to do with it, and the inspector doesn't bother to disagree, he finds her so lackluster as a suspect.

Then the telephone interrupts them and Philippot spends a few minutes paying close attention to the caller, saying little while fresh evidence appears to be on offer at the other end of the line. At last he hangs up and says fine, that's enough for today.

I'm free to go? asks Viviane in surprise.

Right, you're free, replies Yul as he escorts her to the exit, limiting contact with the grateful eyes of the mother and the more cautiously circumspect gaze of the child. You really could have found someone to take care of her, you know, he says a bit more pleasantly.

5

The article in *Le Parisien* the next day, Wednesday, November 17, poses all sorts of problems. According to the paper, the doctor's body was not found until the morning after his death—and not by his wife or a patient but by a green-eyed redhead in an advanced state of pregnancy, a resident of L'Argentière-la-Bessée in the Hautes-Alpes, someone about whom one might well wonder what she was doing there on Tuesday at six thirty a.m. Then there was some difficulty in tracking down Madame Sergent. Although officially residing with her husband in a comfortable apartment on Rue du Pot-de-Fer, she appeared to spend her nights in a two-room flat on Rue du Roi-de-Sicile belonging to one Silverio Da Silva. Who—a psychoanalyst but not a psychiatrist, or even a doctor or state-certified psychologist, in short a simple lay analyst credentialed by

the goodwill of his peers—did not deny being the widow's lover. Instead of getting huffy when the investi-
gators asked him, in their petty bureaucratic way, if it
didn't bother him to borrow another man's wife, he at-
tempted to point out that the human experience cannot
be reduced to the laws of civil society, or rather that one
sometimes enjoys transgressing them. Well naturally,
riposted the public servants as they locked him up for
the night. "Love: You are paying less and less attention
to your look. Success: Avoid decisions that might affect
your future. Health: Allergies."

Viviane finishes her coffee at the café-bar on Rue
Louis-Blanc, where she is beginning to be a regular. She
has a cup there while waiting to pick up her daughter.
It seems that the other mothers are overburdened, delighted to hand off their children in return for an hour
or two of freedom, and Viviane wonders what for, as
there are not enough administrative procedures to take
up an entire life, nor enough creative resources at any
hair salon to justify going there more than once a week.
She closes the paper and winds up back at the intersection, next to the northbound railway tracks of the Gare
de l'Est, which run beneath the elevated métro track.
Thus all the streets in the neighborhood seem spread

out like a fan, held together by the traffic circle where Louis-Blanc intersects Rue Cail, and gathered up at the other end by the metal ribbon of the métro above Boulevard de la Chapelle.

Beneath a sky dimmed by a profusion of bare branches, she veers right, along a strip of foreign grocery stores, Western Union agencies, cheap variety bazaars, butcher shops, and telephone retailers. Groups of Sri Lankan men without Sri Lankan women are deep in discussion at every doorstep. They might comment on the passage of this tall pale woman, so exotic in their eyes, and yet they pay no attention to her when she slips through their ranks, checking out of the corner of an eye to see if she's attracting any looks but no, she remains as invisible to the Sri Lankans as she is to the others, psychoanalyst, police, and all the rest.

You're going to take a stroll for no reason. One of the privileges of your present situation. You are utterly free and God knows it won't last long, all the mothers say so, insisting that at least twenty years of slavery lie ahead of you.

In the variety store windows there are slippers, socks, teapots, coffeepots, skeins of wool, shirts, pajamas,

DVDs of musicals, and rolling luggage, lots of rolling luggage. You have no use for wheeled suitcases. Wherever would you go? Your trips are entirely taken via the Paris public transportation system. Slippers, on the other hand, you might use. Tucked into the rocking chair with your child, you'd find those fuzzy bloodred slip-ons comfy on your bare feet. Or tucked into your cell, gently rocking in your solitude, you'd find them reminiscent of the very rich hours you are busy living, these last moments before the bureaucrats come to their senses and toss you into the hole. You enter a variety store.

The aisles are organized by categories of objects, from the decorative to the utilitarian. At the entrance, little blue-and-mauve mermaids loll on greenish rocks. Near the cash register, it's colorful multipurpose plastic basins, and between the two displays stretches the gamut of kitchen utensils, toilet articles, children's toys, and items for their mothers: sewing kits, sponges, feather dusters, brooms. You pick up a mermaid looking in your direction, turn her from side to side between your thumb and index, wondering how anyone could buy such an ugly object. You put the mermaid back.

She continues to study you from her shelf. A

little nearsightedly, because her eyes have been hastily sculpted by some worker in Southeast Asia who hasn't given much thought to either the intensity or the precision of her gaze. He has simply painted the pupils, but such as they are, these eyes are looking in your direction. You pick up the mermaid again. Posing on her rock, she reminds you vaguely of someone. A thinker on his pedestal. A parrot on its perch. A shrink in his armchair.

It's just about the time when you ought to have been there. Sitting a few yards from him, fiddling with your fingers in search of your absent wedding ring, some valid association that would earn you a good grade. And he would be in his usual place, absorbed in contemplation of the wall behind you. His mitts would be resting on his stomach while he meditated on a cooking recipe or a crossword problem, waiting for you to show yourself worthy of his profession by agreeing to give up your defensive maneuvers in order to become . . .

Become what, exactly.

A subject. One day he'd said subject.

You'd replied verb, direct object.

He'd said you're avoiding it.

What?

The subject.

Subject. You don't understand what that means. You consult the mermaid, she has nothing to say on the matter and neither do you. You had a husband, a job, a child, obligations that piled up from morning till night. The slightest moment of your existence was ruled by necessity, and you could clearly see that it was the same for everyone else, from the receptionists to the CEO of the Biron Concrete Company, from your mother to the babysitter. You had no idea what could be wrong with such well-oiled systems, you were a completely normal person until you were pressured to become who knows what, and now here's the variety store manager interrupting your tête-à-tête with the mermaid.

He wants to know if you're going to buy it (five euros). You were not aware that it isn't good form to try something out before buying it and you tell him so quite readily—and a trifle brusquely—but still, you leave the store with the slippers you'd noticed in the window. They're two big balls of synthetic fur, like a pair of very soft hedgehogs.

At the end of Rue Louis-Blanc, the Sri Lankans give way to a more cosmopolitan population, offering black-market cigarettes or staked out in the middle of the boulevard with their hot-chestnut carts. Musing over these chestnuts, you decide they are a far cry from the ones sold in front of the big department stores on Boulevard Haussmann when you were still a real bourgeoise, shuttling between two plush arrondissements of Paris, in blessed ignorance of this rundown eastern part of the city.

You cross the boulevard, hesitate between the railroad overpass to the right, which would take you back home, and the Gare du Nord bridge to the left, leading toward Barbès-Rochechouart. From there you would make for the 18th arrondissement (subtropical population, street stalls overflowing with inexpensive accessories) or the 9th arrondissement to the south, with its elegant citizens and boutiques dedicated to this enclave of socioprofessional advantage. All this means making choices. An infinity of microdecisions, each presenting major implications. You are in no position to make choices. You are a slave to necessity, a position that suits you quite well, you have never asked for any other.

Across from you is a modest park where poor children and drug dealers take the air. You push open the gate, sit down on a bench in the sun and, taking the slippers from their bag, slip your hands inside them, where they get quietly warm.

You were nice and warm in the shrink's armchair, too. That was three years ago, when you landed there essentially by chance. As usual, you were on your way to work. You still lived in your first solo apartment, Rue Pradier, métro station Pyrénées, which meant you took the 11 line to République, then the 9 to Saint-Philippe-du-Roule. You were neither happy nor unhappy to be going to Biron Concrete: you never asked yourself the question. You had an excellent position in a big company, in charge of all public and in-house promotional activities, brochures, partnership materials, sponsorships, patronage. Your boss had complete confidence in you, you'd made connections throughout the building industry, and you used them. At cocktail parties or seminars, you didn't shy away from chatting up some design engineer. This would play out in one of the hotel rooms reserved for the event and the next morning, you'd both arrive at the nine o'clock meeting all mussed-looking and wink at each other across the conference room. Such behavior was stupid and immature but still, it was fun to rattle your audience and it would also reawaken the interest of Jean-Paul Biron, who over time tended to confuse you with the office furniture.

So: you'd just gotten off the 11 line at République when the tiled walls of the underground corridor suddenly riveted your attention. And then you couldn't see anything anymore except the horizontal ceramic tiles blocking your horizon. You walked up the steps taking passengers to the main correspondence corridor, also accessed by passengers from three other lines. You went with the flow of the crowd, advancing blindly, listening to the roaring in your arteries that drowned out the noise all around you. You reached the croissant shop at the corner where the 9 joins the main passageway. Smelling the nauseating aroma of fast-food croissants, you took a deep breath of this artificial Viennese pastry in an attempt to surface from the depths. When it was your turn, the young vendor in his ridiculous fast-food uniform said yes, madame, what will you have, madame? The other customers began to grow impatient. They were in a hurry to get to work and wasting time, and it took nerve not to know what you want at a croissant shop at nine in the morning, a lady behind you made that thought crystal clear. You looked at her in the hope that a catfight would revive your survival instinct but you didn't see her, all you could see were tiles.

Then the vendor said, so, madame, a croissant, a pain au chocolat, perhaps, are you sure you're all right, madame, because if not I'll call security, no point in causing a panic like this, people have to get to work. You looked at him in supplication with your blind eyes. You would have loved to say a single word of reassurance, to assert that you knew perfectly who you were, where you were going, and what you wanted in the way of Viennese pastry, but your jaw no longer worked. Your lips opened onto a wall of white tiles, and the young man said right, I'm calling for assistance.

Feeling slightly guilty, the lady behind you led you over to the wall and told you to breathe deeply while awaiting help, it will pass, believe me, I'm a social worker, it always goes away. You were able to say thank you and she turned back toward the onlookers with a look of triumph that said I told you so. Then the rescue services of the fire brigade arrived. They asked you the usual questions to which you replied listlessly, they patted you on the shoulder, repeating what the lady had said, that you were simply overtired, that they

were going to take you to the emergency room as a precaution and that you'd be back in shape to go to work
that afternoon. You replied the same thing that everyone says in such circumstances, no, not the emergency
room, and they gently insisted, because what's the point
of putting on a big show unless you're going to go there.
The doctors will get you back on your feet, believe us,
said the firemen, who always say us.

They helped you out of the métro and into their van
to go to the hospital, where you did not feel too proud of
yourself. You were thirty-nine, had a good position, no
reason to complain, and you couldn't begin to fathom
this moment of weakness that already seemed far behind you. But you intended to consult a specialist, since
they said it would be advisable. And that's how you
wound up seeing the doctor.

The plaque at the entrance to his building specifically
says *doctor*. The patient therefore expects to be seen
by the classic health professional sitting at a large desk
graced with a pen stand, an emerald-green opaline glass
lamp, and a prescription pad.

After she has spent ten minutes in the waiting room,
the doctor ushers her into his office. He invites her to

take a seat in a chrome tube armchair, then sits down in another one a good distance away and at a slight angle to the sight line between them. He says nothing. The patient waits for questions that do not come, considers describing the episode that has led her here, then rethinks her options. The décor. She studies the décor to decide whether she can entrust herself to this man, looking for evidence of his integrity. A familiar object, a book she might have read, a little something to cling to.

Next to her stands a table laden with specialized magazines and brochures advising prudence with regard to alcohol and various drugs. In front of her is a chaise longue that seems to serve as a couch. The doctor has seated himself to the left of this chaise, his heavy eyelids turned toward the window blind behind the desk. A mild day is filtering in from the street. It's the beginning of spring, that period so hard to distinguish from autumn. The light is at the halfway point and without a calendar, there's no way of knowing if it's on the upswing or the decline. Between doctor and patient lies a carpet with complicated motifs in reddish-orange tones.

She embarks on a second tour of inspection. Studies the objects on a shelf fixed to the wall over the chaise.

They sit in front of a row of books that don't tell her a thing because they're in German and her first foreign language in school was English, a fact she suddenly feels obliged to mention, and Spanish was the second, professionally more useful than German which only philosophers and composers ever need—although they keep avoiding it, which is proof enough.

Proof of what, says the doctor.

Which closes the first circle of what will endlessly reproduce itself for three years. The patient selects an object in the décor and makes it say what it doesn't say, revealing the fragile mechanism of her unconscious. Of course, this presupposes belief in the little art of Viennese sorcery practiced by the doctor. He himself admits that one must believe in it or else it won't work any better than voodoo would on a congregation of Pentecostalists, and in the beginning the patient doesn't know if she believes in it but she's willing to let herself be convinced.

She's willing because she has noticed a knickknack in front of the German books on the shelf that reminds her of something her mother has. It's made of copper and is of unknown provenance. It has a long spout with a pouring lip and seems designed to contain a liquid such as oil, tea, or coffee. It might even be a funerary urn intended for the ashes of a small animal. A cat, for example. The patient has a mother who has a cat. But she really doesn't see anything interesting about this story, she announces as she bursts into tears.

And now you're crying. You're sobbing on your bench in the little square on Boulevard de la Chapelle where all action ceases. The children in their sandbox stop excavating, their red or blue plastic shovels frozen aloft, while their mothers stop gossiping and the people palavering beneath the chestnut trees stop conducting their obscure transactions. Everyone rushes over to help but you quickly give them the slip. Fleeing toward the tracks of the Gare de l'Est, you pass the post office and the railway bridge. On the boulevard, you're running past variety and grocery stores again, sidewalks cluttered with yams, sweet potatoes, bananas, then there's a kebab place and a café, a bank, and we're back at the Stalingrad métro station.

It's ten to two; Viviane goes to pick up her daughter.

6

There's this child on our hands and we wonder how it happened. The babysitter handed her over without a fuss, pretending to believe that she was our legitimate property. We sneak off with her, hugging the walls all the way to the building on Rue Cail, in case the woman changes her mind. Once safely in the sixth-floor apartment, we settle into the rocking chair and observe the child for a very long time, waiting for a response, a revelation.

Sometimes she looks at us as if she has known us since forever, and we think she's mistaking us for someone else. Or is it that we aren't the ones we think we are: that's a possibility.

We have no idea where she comes from, this being who knows more about us than we would ever suspect, and who yet expects us to take care of her in every way.

To maintain the illusion of familiarity, we must respond to her warbling and she is the one who guides us, shapes our conversation, insists on building up this recalcitrant family connection. And perhaps she is also the one who, in her naked need and tenacity, will carry the day. Thus we will become mother and daughter simply through her stubbornness.

In the middle of the desperately bare room, we reflect upon what we could do to deserve so much love. No doubt we should take decorative action, consult furniture catalogs, acquire bibelots, stir up the fire of our maternal instinct in the warmth of our home. But we do nothing, passive as usual. The child's crying is always at the same low volume; she seems incredibly satisfied with her situation, a miracle that is frightening at first, although delightful upon reflection, leaving us with no other choice than to carry on as before, obeying the strictures of necessity. Feed, get ready, go out, come back, sleep: it's the body alone that moves forward when we have relapsed into mutism.

We think her satisfaction might come from her father, who perhaps bequeathed her the gene of equanimity. That's one explanation. We know him well, though: it's not very plausible.

We have considered the father of Valentine Hermant from many aspects. There is the side of him we saw when we first met and for a while thereafter, when simply recalling his name sparked the desire to throw all clothing out the window and run to him. There is the perspective of recent days, when he pronounced the definitive words we know, and between these two points lie various intermediary states linked to different factors: the vagaries of his moods, the progress then decline of his affection for us. From one autumn to the next, passing through all the colors of the year.

It was in this very season that we met. After we began seeing the doctor, unexpected events took place. We enjoy remembering those already distant times, but not the intrusion of this telephone now vibrating in our pocket. We answer it. Inspector Philippot is asking for a prompt appearance at the police headquarters of the 5th arrondissement because he has a few more questions to ask you.

7

The second time, the bloom is always off the rose. However risky the situation might still seem and even if the stakes are higher, the modus operandi is locked in. It's all a done deal: the routine, the little idiosyncrasies, the question/answer contests to see who'll come out on top. It's practically a bore already.

Viviane holds the baby close throughout the entire trip to the police station. The child's eyes are wide open but she's quiet, perfectly content to be an amulet, a protective fetish against evil. She registers the elements of the landscape (nippy breeze, encroaching darkness, crowded métro car, curtain of dark coats forming a surrounding well) then turns toward her fists, inexplicably muffled in mittens. Her mother is deciphering advertisements: mattress clearance sales, evening courses, adult English classes, mathematics for grades six through twelve. My daughter, she thinks proudly, will never need remedial courses. She takes after me, it's obvious: she hardly ever cries.

This time they send her up to the fifth floor of the police station, which proves to be a lot more spacious than the fourth. The corridor serves half as many offices and there are no policemen in uniform. Through the blue-tinted glazed partitions, Viviane can see solemn men ballasted by a long career of overly rich lunches.

Philippot is waiting for her at the office door and casts a cool eye at the bundle slung in a scarf around her neck. You really feel this is the proper place for a child? he asks testily. You really feel this is the proper place for me? says Viviane, blushing immediately. Sorry, I'm touchy these days, my husband's left me. The inspector is about to reply but decides not to, stepping aside to let her pass. Behind the desk sits a big bald man quietly picking his teeth.

So, says the fat man, how's it going, my dear little Madame Hermant? I'm Chief Inspector Bertrand. No, don't look so scared, I'm just a chief inspector, not the divisional detective inspector. Him you'll see later on. Maybe. What I mean is, I hope not, Madame Hermant. But of course that depends on you.

I'm not scared at all, says Viviane, who speaks right up like an idiot, that's a trick of the trade, people answer off the tops of their heads even though they'd been determined not to let anything slip about their guilty consciences.

Well of course, you have nothing to reproach yourself for, replies the chief inspector in a tone that means I've already heard that one a million times. We called your mother.

Yes?

It isn't a good idea, Madame Hermant, to play the fool with me. But that's your lookout; you're the one who'll pay for it.

You called my mother, replies Viviane, looking the chief inspector straight in the eye.

Yes, Madame Hermant, we called your mother. And she's dead, your mother. She died on February 16, 2002, so she's been dead a good eight years, therefore I just don't see how she could have confirmed that you did not kill Dr. Jacques Sergent on November 15, 2010. Naturally, I might conclude, since you spend your life at this doctor's office, that you're utterly nuts. But we also called your husband, Monsieur Julien Hermant, and your employer, Monsieur Jean-Paul Biron. They have described you as beyond reproach as a wife and employee, so I must urge you most emphatically, Madame Hermant, to provide us with a few explanations.

Even though everyone tells you that I'm beyond reproach? sneers the accused. Yes, my mother died on February 16, 2002: I'm almost certain of the date—I've got a pretty good memory for dates.

Your mother, continues the chief inspector, massaging his temples, owned an apartment on Place Saint-Médard in the 5th arrondissement, near the Censier-Daubenton métro station.

Excuse me, she still owns it. I pay the bills, the property tax, I go there once a month to do the windows and the dusting, I never canceled the phone.

So you're the one who owns that apartment.

Yes, I'm the one, she's the one, split hairs if you want. Put it this way: we own the apartment. What is it you're trying to say, Chief Inspector?

You're playing with matches.

What can I say? I haven't been able to make up my mind to sell it or rent it out. I was waiting for the right moment, that's what I was working on with the doctor. My husband understood very well.

That's not what he told us.

And just what did he say?

He said that if you had sold the apartment, which is worth around nine hundred euros per square foot, you would have had about a million in your piggybank. He added that this would have avoided the necessity of renting that three-room apartment on Rue Louis-Braille, but he was careful to insist that he was not thinking about the money but about your comfort together as a family. Regarding the doctor, we can therefore eliminate any financial motive.

Viviane studies the chief inspector's features closely: heavy eyelids, fleshy mouth, double chin, and the wrinkles of concentration that hold everything together. She decides he doesn't believe she could be the murderer.

I did not kill the doctor, she sighs. I'm not going to fabricate such a thing, after all. I was home with my daughter; I did not kill the inspector.

You mean the doctor.

I mean the doctor.

Why did you suggest that we call your mother?

I don't know, it just popped out. That's what the doctor taught me, to speak without thinking too much about it.

We're not in the doctor's office, Madame Hermant.

Listen, I grant you that you're going through a difficult time at the moment, with the divorce and everything. But this business of saying things to detectives off the top of your head, keeping an apartment worth a million without realizing any return whatsoever—it's just no good. You have to get a grip or there'll be repercussions. Now go on, beat it.

That's not what she'd expected: too easy, sounds like a trap, and humiliating, too. Viviane glances from the chief inspector to Philippot, who has been standing in a corner since the beginning of the interview, a tall, slinky, elegant silhouette leaning against the glass partition. She notes absentmindedly the lines of his clothing, observes again how impatient the chief inspector is as he snatches up the toothpick where he abandoned it on the blotter a little while ago. Then, as there is nothing more to say, she gathers up her things, leaves the room mumbling something inaudible, and heads down the hall.

Sitting on the edge of a plastic chair, a very pregnant woman with red hair is fiddling nervously with her nails. Viviane recognizes her immediately from having studied her picture in the morning paper. The young woman does not notice Viviane, however. She's looking for someone else and when she sees the inspector, who

has come out into the hall, she's found him. She has returned of her own accord, yes, she would like to speak
to the police again, to help with the investigation, and
has remembered a few things that might interest them.
After Philippot has ushered her into the office, Viviane
finds herself alone with her daughter, who is still saying
nothing but whose eyes are heavy with reproach.

8

After that I don't know why I do what I do, but I do it. Not that I believe it's a good idea or that I'm proud of myself, only—I have to: my feet go forward and I follow them.

I leave the police station. Night encloses Boulevard Saint-Germain; passersby hasten toward the métro entrance. It's easy to interpret their movements. I could be any one of them, going home from work, swinging by the day care center, and I'd stop off at the supermarket for a few things before jumping on a bus where someone would let me have his seat. I'd get home, warm up the bottle while my husband would give the baby a bath, then we'd sit in front of the television, eating a frozen dinner I'd heated up, and toddle off to bed without making love, unless it's the evening when we do make love, in which case we'd sleep better, before beginning again the cycle of days, weeks, years, safe from all suspicion.

Appearances are on my side. Equipped with that alibi, I head toward Rue des Écoles, where I know I will find a hotel. Indeed, I find several. They're lined up parallel to the Seine on the uneven-numbers side of the street, but I doubt that one can glimpse, from behind the pastel curtains of these semiluxurious establishments, the river and its tourist attractions: Notre Dame, the former royal palace and prison of the Conciergerie, the headquarters of the Police Judiciaire in Paris at Quai des Orfèvres, and the courts of the Palais de Justice. I have my plan. I need a hotel room for a few hours, something not too costly because I'm not sure if I'll have additional expenses later on and I'd like to economize.

As it happens, these hotels all have three or four stars. Prices are not posted at the door and I don't dare go inside to ask about them, not wanting to seem hard up. Finally I stop in front of the Moderne Saint Germain where I overhear the conversation of a very East Coast American couple: they will go to the Louvre rather than on the Bateaux-Mouches excursion boats, will skip the Moulin Rouge in favor of the Musée d'Orsay. I don't need to know them to guess everything about their itinerary because I'd do the same in their place. When I was a girl, I too enjoyed discovering new places by sticking to the sites recommended in travel guides. I smile at the couple and glance inside the hotel; a discreet-looking young man is standing at the reception desk. It's exactly what I need. But first, a drugstore.

There's one close by, where I wait on line at the pharmacy and examine the analgesics and sedatives on display behind the counter. They're mostly antihistamines, phytotherapeutic capsules, which wouldn't put a horse to sleep but a thirteen-pound child, no problem. When it's my turn, I ask for four different boxes and, as a precaution, I produce my doctor's prescription so that I can obtain the tranquilizers, just the tranquilizers. The young pharmaceutical intern gives me a worried look but I don't back down. I am the customer, she is not a policewoman, I stare back at her until she hurries off to fetch my pills, then I return to the Moderne Saint Germain where I book a single room. It's seventy-seven euros.

The receptionist as well would like me to be forthcoming with explanations. He doesn't ask for them but I can tell from his sidelong glances that I should invent a story to justify swanning in with a three-month-old child as my only luggage. So I claim to be from Nevers in Burgundy, my car has broken down and won't be ready until tomorrow morning. It's at the Mercedes dealership on the corner I add, because a big car always inspires confidence. He visibly relaxes and, handing me the key to the room, wishes me good night. I say thank you.

The room contains the bare minimum of furniture, plus pink-and-green curtains. Extracting a drawer from a chest, I line it with towels and settle the baby inside. She's still not asleep, still not crying, and looks at me as if to say, old thing, whatever are you up to now? Sometimes I feel as if she were the mother and I the child, and I reflect that in this case, there's no point in giving her the pills I bought: she won't betray me. As if to agree with me, she closes her eyes and goes to sleep.

While the receptionist is sorting through his brochures for the Americans, I leave the Moderne Saint Germain and go back toward Place Maubert, where I park myself in a café practically next door to the police station. In this morning's *Le Parisien* I study the photo of the young redhead who showed up earlier to offer new information to the detectives: I want to be sure I recognize her when she comes walking along from Rue des Carmes. Then I withdraw into myself and explore the memory of her face glimpsed in the hall of the police station, gathering all the elements at my disposal so I won't blow my fleeting chance.

Which occurs shortly after nine o'clock. On the other side of the boulevard, a compact mass is moving against the flow of traffic, weaving among the metal frames set up for the market tomorrow. Weighed down by the burden of her belly, her steps are further slowed by the confusion affecting both her mind and body. She advances in jolts, reconsiders, stops in a bus shelter to study the maps of transport lines, and sets out again in a westward direction. I leave the café, skirt the fountain—keeping my prey in sight as she moves slowly in a corner of my visual field—and trail her without any exaggerated precautions. An icy November rain is falling, infiltrating the seams of shoes, chilling legs up to the knees, and will render useless all later attempts to warm up.

Having reached the Saint-Michel bridge, the young woman once again considers the possibility of public transport, which here offers a much larger selection of options—métro, bus, Regional Express Network—but she decides to keep walking, and now we're crossing the bridge. I do not like bridges. I do not like where we're headed, the police headquarters at Quai des Orfèvres and its vans all parked in front of us, headlights off, staring at me with dead eyes. But we walk past the police building, the spear-tipped fence outside the courthouse, the flank of the Conciergerie, crossing the Île de la Cité to reach the bridge on the other side where I can breathe better—it must be the fresh air over the river—and I hang back so as not to pass the woman still walking quietly along in front of me because suddenly I would like to run, having escaped the ancient stone walls of the Île de la Cité.

The young woman is not in so much of a hurry. She walks toward Rue de Rivoli, loiters a moment in front of a brightly illuminated shoe boutique, then proceeds up Boulevard de Sébastopol, turning right when abreast of the Centre Pompidou. I fear my plan has come undone when she goes over to a keypad door lock, but she turns around and heads for a brasserie. Guessing her intention, I dart off to the left and just beat her to the door. Entering, I allow myself a glance around.

The solitary customers are lined up along the banquette, facing a television showing a soccer match with the sound turned down. Most of the tables are occupied but I spy two that are free, side by side near the bar, and I take a seat at one—the table closest to a radiator—without looking at the person who has just come in after me. The three plasticized panels of the menu offer various meats with french fries or the usual vegetable sides.

I'll have the steak, I tell the waiter who comes to take my order and, using this occasion to look up from my menu, I pretend to notice the round belly of the young woman now seated to my left. I am flustered: wouldn't she rather sit near the radiator?

Oh no, she feels warm, so warm that the last thing she wants is to be closer to the radiator. She thanks me nevertheless, says she's touched by my concern, because you can't imagine how people can play blind on a bus, deliberately ignoring the huge belly looming over the barrier of crossword pages they erect to protect their jump seats. I can imagine quite well I say, delighted because Angèle—that's her name, she introduces herself first thing—is in the mood to chat.

People think that the victims of tabloid tragedies are left stupefied, ashamed. Actually, they ask only to speak. They need witnesses to corroborate what they have seen and to recognize the injury done to them. The young woman leans her face over to me, with that milky complexion so typical of redheads, her big eyes gleaming with provincial candor. Angèle wants to share, and anyone at all would fill the bill. I am a shadow, a vessel, I say pleased to meet you, I'm Élisabeth.

9

You are the collateral victim of a sensational incident and you cannot get over it. As far as you're concerned, the world fell apart Tuesday morning when you discovered the inanimate body of the doctor lying in his office to which you happened to have the key. Since then you have been wandering in a field of ruins, waiting for an equally supernatural phenomenon to put everything back to rights.

You are twenty-six. Born in the département des Hautes-Alpes, you still live there officially, with your parents, but have been living in Paris since getting your baccalaureate. You move from one room to another as your university years go by, paying the rent with your stipend (your family is a large one with only modest resources) and what you can earn from odd seasonal jobs.

You are now a doctoral student. Before his brutal death, you were very close to your thesis director.

Meaning what? asks Élisabeth, fishing for details.

You don't avoid the issue; you would like your audience to fully understand the situation and thus guide you, perhaps, toward an angle from which you might otherwise never have viewed things, and from which the image would recompose itself as if in an anamorphosis.

Five years ago you set out to seduce a professor whose old-fashioned, even faded air had somehow touched you. You've always had strange tastes. Your peers ignored him in favor of more obvious specimens, the university stars who played nonchalantly on their prestige, shining in the brilliance of their thoughts and dramatically flinging out their arms to wave their eyeglasses in the air for emphasis. You'd been the only one to bet on Professor Sergent, never hearing a word of the lectures he delivered so doggedly because you were too busy admiring him through half-closed eyes. And your imagination began running away with you so much that you soon had to stifle your daydreams: in the silence of the auditorium, you were afraid of letting slip too eloquent a sigh.

For months you waited at the foot of the dais to ask insignificant questions, leaving more and more pregnant pauses until he suggested continuing the conversation at a café, where the discussion mainly featured throat-clearing and eyelash-batting. It took a complete campaign to prompt an invitation to a restaurant and months more of effort to wangle an appointment at the doctor's office, after consultation hours.

Neglected by his wife, Jacques had precious little experience of love. You have tender memories of his chubby fingers probing the openings in your clothes, hardly daring to venture further. No, the doctor was not really at ease with women, aside from a few flings with patients at the end of their cure, when through sheer boredom doctor and patient had thrown themselves at each other just for something to do. He had observed that this technique significantly accelerated the resolution of transference. After three weeks they would be seeing each other less and less and after two months, not at all. But whenever you came up with some objection, armed with the convictions of your age and the principles inculcated by the university, he would wax ironic about the fanaticism of youth to disparage your arguments. And you, busy shedding your clothes on the chaise to foster a more direct approach to the subject, had come away rather disappointed. Disappointed and pregnant, which you now illustrate by pointing a finger at your belly jammed against the table on which your frankfurters and fries have just been placed, while your neighbor, sitting with her now cold steak and ratatouille, considers you with the stunned amazement of someone who has never before encountered the victim of a sensational incident.

You're off and running now, you spare her nothing. You describe how the doctor took the news (up on his high horse, as if he'd never gotten anywhere near her), how he made fun of young Angèle Trognon (that's your name), announcing point-blank that he wasn't going to leave his wife for a student.

It's a girl? asks Élisabeth suddenly.

It *is* a girl. How did you know that?

Just a thought.

You observe your neighbor, who still hasn't touched her food. You could take an interest in her now, ask if she has children, inquire about her situation. You couldn't care less about all that. And since you've finished the saga of your misadventures, you tackle your present experience, the relentless harassment that leaves you no time to bemoan your fate. The authorities are pressing you about your intentions, about questions of money and inheritance. Bank statements must be produced, expenses justified—you have no idea, you tell Élisabeth, what questions you get asked after a crime.

Well, replies Élisabeth, who is languidly picking the eggplant out of her ratatouille with the tip of her knife, I think I should be going.

You have worn out your audience. There she is putting on her gray coat, dropping a bill on the table without waiting for her change or saying good-bye. The coat sails across the room—sweeping the tables, destroying in its wake any forks and breadbaskets in precarious equilibrium at their tables' edges—and out of the café, bound for its mysterious destination. You will learn nothing more about the woman who listened to you. Her face is already dwindling in your memory and you have even forgotten her name.

This woman is now walking back along Boulevard de Sébastopol toward the taxi stand at Châtelet. There she takes a Mercedes that reaches Rue des Écoles in eight minutes. Without bothering to whip up an explanation for the young reception clerk, she goes up to room 17 and walks in at 11:09 p.m.: it has been exactly a hundred and twenty minutes since she left the baby, who is just waking up. Viviane carries her away in the taxi still waiting downstairs.

I O

Le Parisien announces the next day that the widow is being held by the police. There's a photo with the article, showing her escorted by two uniformed officers at the entrance to police headquarters. She's a woman of about fifty, slender, elegant; the doctor must have made a good living. I try to get a reading on her character but it's a snapshot taken on the fly, printed on cheap newsprint. It reveals nothing except that the woman would no doubt prefer to be elsewhere, nibbling on a pastry in a tearoom or visiting art galleries with her girlfriends while their husbands work in their opulent offices. The article simply says that the police suspect her because she was leading a double life, Rue du Roi-de-Sicile, with that Silverio Da Silva, the man they recently arrested but released.

Then the following day brings a new twist. In

connection with this affair they are now interrogating one Tony Boujon, twenty-three, a printing-plant
worker. A patient of the doctor's, but one with a police
record. Toward the end of spring, armed with a knife,
he'd attacked a girl outside the Lycée Paul-Valéry as
she was leaving the school. Detectives had searched
the room he still lived in at home with his parents, on
Rue Montgallet in the 12th arrondissement, whereupon
they'd discovered that this young man owned a lovely
collection of knives.

In short, the widow is free, and I immediately take up
my post on Rue du Roi-de-Sicile. I had no trouble ob-
taining the address. Shoved to the front of the stage, the
protagonists of police-blotter dramas have not had time
to get an unlisted number: they're all in the phone book.
And on the Internet it's child's play to locate their block
on a city map, cruise over it, and even get an idea of their
building's façade. In the end I managed to pick out a
nearby front porch where I could stand guard.

Just as I was ready to go about my business my
daughter rose in revolt, and this time I didn't hesitate
to put her to sleep. I gave her a quarter of one of those
tablets you are not supposed to administer to children

under six. But I know these drugs: the best they can do is induce a vague drowsiness. Then I left the apartment after turning the radiators up full blast. I like my daughter to be cozy.

The cold is seeping between my ears. At times I must step aside to let someone pass and I use my cell phone to make myself less conspicuous. I pretend to text an important message but as usual, no one notices me. I'm a thing they walk by, an obstacle to be avoided, and I've no idea how long I'll have to play the lookout here.

Thick flakes begin to fall. They win out against the asphalt, soon carpeting every aspect of the landscape: ledges, branches, cornices, flowerpots, windshield wipers at rest, recycling bins, transparent green plastic garbage bags, cardboard boxes, bulk trash. To pass the time and take my mind off the cold, I make mental note of the places infiltrated by the snow. I'm not properly shod for this climate; I didn't bring my gloves or check the weather report, either. I've had so much to think about lately.

Shifting from one foot to the other, I consider calling off my vigil. The widow will probably not go out today. I put myself in her place. Wrung out by events, I'd stay well away from the windows, huddled in an armchair to chew my guilt down to the bone, and would now live exclusively off my fierce resentment. I would let myself go, wear threadbare clothes, stop tweezing and grow a unibrow above my nose.

Toward the middle of the afternoon, however, she ventures outside. I can tell right away that I don't like her kind of woman. Haughty in her furs and her blond coiffure, she looks like a White Russian. Her heels tap lightly along the sidewalk as she moves delightedly through the snow. Trailing behind at a pace somewhat numbed by my wait, I follow her onto Rue de Turenne, where I must struggle not to lose ground. The flakes are falling ever faster, blurring contours, and I bump into passersby, twisting my ankles on stroller wheels. I'm not a bad walker, but the doctor's wife seems borne along by the wind while I'm buffeted by its twists and turns.

She enters a café on the corner of Turenne and Bretagne, looking around for a man she finds at the far end of the room with his back to a mirror. I sit two tables away and concentrate on the voices of the woman, wearing a tight black dress, and the man, who is either really handsome or absolutely not.

The widow is very agitated, with lots of things to say all at once. Her companion must constantly interrupt her to clarify details essential to the whole story.

But really the only thing he's interested in is how it turns out. He wants to know where they stand with the cops. Anyone would want to know that, me first of all, and the doctor's wife is doing her best to drive us crazy.

Calm down, she keeps saying without answering any of his questions, you're not letting me talk, let me tell you or you can just go read it in the papers.

I've read the papers. It's police custody one after the other, first Silverio and then you, and I tell myself the police don't hold people without having some kind of idea in the back of their heads. So explain to me what's going on.

But you can see they're just fishing, she says smiling. They try out one fish, they toss it back into the water. And they come up with such words, I swear, nobody talks like that. *Flighty, passion, legacy*—you'd think you were trapped in a provincial melodrama. Which reminds me, did you know that Angèle came from the Alps? Then she turns silently to the mirror to fine-tune the unstructured structure of her hairdo. That done, it's a gift from heaven, she continues, his having this old mistress.

She's half your age, points out the man.

Old: around for a long time, replies the widow airily. Old: old school, she free-associates. Poor Jacques.

Sleeping with a student. I mean who sleeps with their students anymore?

Plenty of people, replies the man in irritation. Me, for example.

Right, she says in a determined tone, it's time for you to go. Give Mama a kiss for me.

I'm certainly glad I came, he concludes, with a look that says otherwise. At least I'm used to it.

The widow watches him coldly while he puts on his jacket and vanishes into the snow, and I decide that there is in fact a certain similarity between the two of them. The same pale skin, the same silvery blond hair, the same bland features, but the configuration of these features is entirely different: in her case they form a harmonious composition, whereas in his they dash off in all directions to create a chaotic tangle. Then the widow moves into his empty place on the banquette and picks up an afternoon paper, one of those that doesn't set much store by vulgar crime cases.

I must speak to her. She's right there in front of me, as if nothing extraordinary had ever happened lately, the wife of the man to whom I confided everything. I rise and approach her, full of humility, saying excuse me, I'm sorry to disturb you, I'm a friend of Angèle's.

The widow sizes me up with her gray eyes.

Yes? she says, dragging out the *s*, reluctant to grant me a hearing.

I keep going, on instinct: I'd like to speak to you—what I mean is, Angèle asked me to speak to you.

You followed me?

A little, I have to admit blushingly, but don't worry, I didn't hear any of your conversation.

Doesn't matter, my brother's an ass. So, you're following me?

I can tell that she feels flattered in some obscure way, so I sit down. My name is Élisabeth I say, holding out my hand.

You may call me Gabrielle she sighs, without extending hers.

So I take a running start and leap into the void.

Here's the thing: Angèle thought that it might be possible to come to an arrangement. She has nothing to do with this business—this terrible business, I add prudently—and she is convinced that you don't, either. Your husband often spoke to her about you, and she admires you greatly. (Gabrielle strokes her satiny cheekbones with a dreamy expression.) Angèle, I continue, has no desire to start a lawsuit. She knows that she has no right to anything, but she's young and there's the child to bring up.

So that's all any of you ever think about—the money? snaps Gabrielle in sudden irritation.

I don't know, I reply humbly. Money, love—we take the one when we can't have the other, don't you think?

The widow considers this observation as if wondering what her due is, of money and love, and seems to come to a conclusion distinctly in her favor for she's smiling again, the smile she uses with photographers.

And you, who are you? she asks, catching me off guard.

A friend. A friend from the Alps, I say quickly. And up there we're rather informal, I add, hoping that this will somewhat excuse my behavior.

It is obvious that you aren't from around here.

I swallow my pride, but the truth is I no longer have any. I am the plaything of circumstances and I've decided not to resist, to go whichever way the wind blows. I hear myself reply you're right, my manners are dreadful, and we often thought, Angèle and I, that we'd like to be more like you.

Well, the unfortunate Jacques never mentioned Angèle to me at all, still less you, she says for her own amusement. I was aware of her existence, of course, but he was hardly going to boast about it. Would you like to hear my story? she adds, moved by a sudden inspiration.

Née Sherbatoff fifty-two years ago, Gabrielle had opted for medical school. Yet she had not met her husband there but in the waiting room of their famous mentor, who was always mixing up his appointments. So instead of enjoying privacy, his patients often found themselves waiting with three or four others. Gabrielle dropped medicine because Jacques already had his degree plus an active and prosperous practice.

Her husband thought that she would commit herself completely to the care and cultivation of his daily life, which he dedicated to his practice and research. Freed from all household responsibilities, he would be able to fully deploy the great breadth of his theories, exploring the shadowy zones of the psyche, and he would always have a kind word at the end of the day for his spouse, to thank her for her generous support and tireless devotion.

Mistake. Gabrielle would refuse energetically to don such an unenviable straitjacket, and the doctor would never rival his mentor: known for his stubborn and excessive adherence to the rules, Dr. Jacques Sergent would be called upon to settle administrative problems and deal with unpopular decisions, but his work would never inspire a symposium or a special edition of any journal. He was cited for courtesy's sake in bibliographies.

As for Gabrielle, although she paid scant attention to her domestic surroundings, she was fastidious about her person and in particular about her mind. Once she had settled the problem of her financial upkeep, she went from seminar to seminar, expanding her horizons, and even dared to publish two or three articles that were quite favorably received. This did not sit well with the doctor. Then he considered how he might turn this situation to his advantage. Having given up on advancing his career through his own efforts, he set up a little arrangement with his wife: he would continue to support her, while in return Gabrielle agreed to write up a few case studies under his name. Their relationship thus dwindled away without ever breaking off. They would meet every Sunday at the Rue du Pot-de-Fer apartment to discuss current projects and pay bills, after which they would part in excellent spirits, Gabrielle returning to Silverio Da Silva and Jacques to his own routine.

◆

While I hide my trembling hands under the table, Gabrielle is now silent. Smiling, very proud of herself. I grab the metal center post of the table and squeeze it until my palms burn. I start pinching my knees and feel my nails through the cloth of my pant legs, then I attack my thighs, which does help me calm down. Gradually I relax and feel like myself again. I bring my hands out from under the table and pour the tea that has just arrived.

Quite a story I remark, to show my detachment.

Like it? replies the widow. In that case, you need simply pass it on to your friend Angèle. Or I can relay it myself, if you give me her phone number. But above all, about the money, not a chance.

I haven't got my cell phone, it has all the numbers I say, looking at Gabrielle, and I take a sip of tea, which gives me time to think because I immediately remember that I placed my cell on the empty chair to my left. As I'm putting my cup down I see her looking away from the phone and back at my lying face. But I straighten up while pushing away the hand grabbing at my sleeve and I shove her back when she rises to detain me by force. Snatching up my phone I leave the café posthaste.

I I

Viviane, think of your career.* You know that you're not twenty anymore and that young women are lying in ambush, ready to take your place and wring your neck. Perhaps they're already installed in your big office on Rue de Ponthieu, where they've let your ferns die, thrown out all your fountain pens, replaced your posters of the Florentine masters with photos of carnivorous flowers like sundew and bladderwort, and soon you will have ceased to exist.

You also know that you do not deserve your 4,500 euros net per month. You've hit your maximum, you've got nothing more to offer Biron Concrete. For years they've been keeping you purring in your office, with

---

* Throughout this chapter, the narrative voice addresses Viviane with the familiar pronoun *tu* instead of the formal *vous*.—Trans.

its wide selection of particleboard furniture in different shades of gray that watches you daydream as you pretend to think up presentations, sprinkle punctuation around brochures, set up websites.

Viviane, reclaim your position. At your age and with offspring you're not going to start again at zero, climbing the steps of humiliation from the bottom of the ladder. There isn't enough room for everybody. Well, you've got your job and you're going to defend it. Your daughter will not witness her mother unemployed, besieging social agencies, counting small change tossed into a plastic cup while passengers wrinkle their noses at the aroma you leave behind in the métro car.

Héloïse is the person you hired to fill in for you during your maternity leave. Héloïse studied public relations in an excellent university, has a stellar portfolio, and she can spell. All you could pounce on during her two-week trial period at the beginning of the summer were a few ill-advised past participles here and there, but it was a pleasure to correct them with showy manifestations of indulgence. The two of you got along fairly well. Which was in your joint interest because Jean-Paul Biron was watching you both out of the corner of his eye, while *you* were watching right back. You had to make sure he wasn't too taken with Héloïse's fuselage, so that once you'd delivered this child pummeling your hips, you wouldn't have too much trouble reclaiming your role as the reigning favorite.

Today is November 22, a Monday, and it's high time to take stock. You're wearing a belted raincoat over a blouse with a most flattering neckline and black pants just a tad roomy. Facing the mirror, you felt that the ensemble reasonably emphasized your return to form and recovered allure. Yes Viviane, you can still pull it off on Place de l'Étoile and pass for a high-class tart among misinformed tourists.

You swing through the revolving door at Biron Concrete with a triumphant step, raising a wave of rejoicing behind the reception desk, for the two young women there harbor certain reservations vis-à-vis Héloïse, who is their age but has better diplomas, plus pretensions and attitudes that encourage a desire to see her canned. You hide your pleasure behind a sympathetic mask. But take heart, girls: within three weeks, you'll be firmly back in charge, and ambitious young things will simply have to beat a retreat.

As it happens, not everyone thinks that Héloïse's personality is a wrench in the works for the company.

Jean-Paul Biron for example—who receives you in the fourth-floor conference room because painters are at work in his office—is proud of the contributions the young woman has made to the managerial style he envisions for the coming year, a particularly dynamic, enterprising approach that's more open to diversity.

And just what are you suggesting, Jean-Paul?

Oh, nothing specific for the moment, but I thought that with your new responsibilities . . .

Yes, Jean-Paul? you inquire in a murderous tone.

Well, we might hire this young, uh, what's her name again, Héloïse, yes, to help you out a little?

Help me out a little with what, Jean-Paul? With my work? My career? My life?

Okay okay, we'll drop the subject. She'll go on the dole like everyone else. Otherwise, I was thinking of moving you up to the top floor to be closer to me. What do you say to that?

Viviane, what do you say, you say nothing. In any case, it will still be footbridges and subway tunnels, traffic circles and highways, excavators and backhoes.

Come, I'd like to show you something, continues Jean-Paul, pulling you toward the elevator.

You go down to the first basement. Before reaching the general services department, which is a fancy name for some broom closets, you turn off toward a room that has been freshly refurbished. On something like a billiard table sits a miniature village with its main street, its church on the village square, its monument to the war dead. The details are rendered with an especially realistic touch, such as the baguettes with their ridged crusts on display in the bakery, the geraniums in the windows, the carafes on the bistro tables.

Yes? you say encouragingly, half wheedling, half prying, the way one deals with a patient suspected of having a serious personality disorder.

Héloïse did it, announces Jean-Paul, beaming. To show we don't just disfigure the landscape, that we also renew our national heritage. To present our policy of sustainable development in a good light, you see?

Frankly, you don't see at all. On the other hand, you get the idea someone had a lot of time on her hands, after you'd been careful to leave Héloïse with impressive stacks of files to keep her busy.

Well, hedges Jean-Paul, it's mostly for show, of course. Because we're not going to start sprucing up

villages for communities in financial straits. Those big
tower buildings are still more profitable. But this is
pretty, don't you think?

Magnificent, you say firmly, heading back to the
elevator.

Then you tour the offices to say hello to your colleagues, collecting congratulations from the mothers,
envious or sympathetic smiles from the young women,
and polite indifference from the gentlemen. They've
taken up a collection and present you with a big package
wrapped in paper sprinkled with stylized infants. To
yourself you exclaim what is this ghastly thing, to them
oh how wonderful. When you solve the mystery it turns
out to be a coatrack: the hooks are formed by the trunks
of the elephants down at the base. You thank everyone
again, kiss everyone again, and dash off to your office.

She's sly, Héloïse. She welcomes you all smiles and
practically curtsies, with her blue eyes and silken curls.
She's pleased to see you, tells you straight-out. You don't
believe a word. You see that your ferns are still there—
but luxuriant, glowing with health. They've been
appropriated, lavished with care. A mother wouldn't
recognize her own ferns. And it's even your slightest

talents that are thus devalued, to increase your feeling of superfluity.

Héloïse, let's go over my files, you announce without any more preamble. But of course everything is in order: not one e-mail unanswered, not one phone call forgotten. Show me my brochures, you say next. The young woman explains that they've just arrived from the printer's and there hasn't been time to unpack them. You slash open the blister packaging with a letter opener and feverishly scan the introduction in which Jean-Paul describes the relative merits of bituminous concrete, self-compacting concrete, fibrous concrete, prestressed concrete, and cyclopean concrete; at the twenty-second line you hit pay dirt: *grannulometric spectra* has an extra *n*. You collapse onto a chair, fainting with relief.

They suggest having lunch together, but you'd rather take a little advantage of your freedom. See you very soon, Jean-Paul; good luck with your job search, Héloïse. Your eviscerated gift package under your arm, you head for the Champs-Élysées where you pay brief attention to the Christmas decorations before noticing the crowd gathered in front of the Vuitton boutique. So over you go as well to see if there's something new in the window. But the objects are stamped with their usual brand logo, and perhaps that's what the passersby have come to check on, to see if values still hold firm, that the International Prototype Meter still resides in Paris.

In the pocket of your raincoat, the phone begins to vibrate. After a moment's hesitation you fish it out and see the name Julien Hermant on the screen.

It's me, he announces uselessly.

I can see that it's you you reply, jostling your way out of the crowd.

How are things going, Viviane?

Not well at all, as you can imagine.

Julien clears his throat, says I spoke to the police.

I know, they told me.

I said that you were a wonderful person and that you would never have done such a thing.

Obviously I would never have done such a thing.

I insisted on the fact that you were a very good mother and very professional at work. That in spite of all our differences I still had complete confidence in you.

That's fine, Julien, you said what was needed.

Now I'd like you to take back the cat.

A little silence falls. Then you reply I took the child, you can at least keep the cat.

I don't want the cat, says Julien. I want my daughter, every other weekend and during the vacations.

You're not going to start all that again.

We have to see each other Viviane, we have to talk. That's what people do.

You think it over. You say all right, we'll see each other on Sunday. I'll go to my mother's to do a bit of cleaning, you can join me there.

I'd rather it be elsewhere.

I don't feel like arguing.

Okay then, replies Julien.

1 2

All gangling limbs, Tony Boujon looks out at me through his too-long bangs: a young man whose story is easy to guess. From neglectful parents to keeping bad company, the natural faults of childhood confirmed by the pressure of toxic influences, he has developed the character of a little creep and inspires no sympathy. In the spring he followed a girl for several weeks before accosting her with a knife one day outside her school, but the intended victim just stared at him with her big round eyes until he backed down and put away his knife, all ardor squelched. He got three months in jail, a suspended sentence of two years, plus mandatory psychiatric treatment.

I called out to him at the Gare de l'Est at 8:31 a.m. as he was getting off the commuter train on his way home from his job. Tony Boujon works in a printing plant in Lagny-Thorigny. His shift begins at midnight and ends at dawn. In the pale light sifting down from the glass canopy of the train station, I could immediately pick out his skinny form among the other passengers. I stepped in front of him with a big smile and said you're Tony Boujon.

He gaped at me like a carp.

I repeated you're Tony Boujon, I saw your photo in the newspaper, I think I can help you.

Help me with what, he snapped, I didn't do anything, and who are you anyway, I already talked to the police.

How about some coffee? I suggested while leading him gently toward an exit.

We chose a rather dark place on Boulevard de Strasbourg.

Tony chews on his ink-blackened nails while I stroke my glossy manicured fingertips.

My name is Élisabeth I begin, without getting him to look up. He makes a show of yawning, begins fiddling studiously with the seams of one of his sneakers and I press on saying I know, yes, I know that you were one of the doctor's patients.

The boy looks up in spite of himself.

He wasn't much help, was he? I add with a complicitous wink, and in passing I graze his knee with mine under the table. Tony straightens up like a shot in his seat, his long bangs flopping limply down on his forehead furrowed with dismay. I say sorry, it's a reflex: we nurses are so used to touching people we don't even notice anymore. So he relaxes, his lips almost ready to crack a smile. A nurse, he's fine with that. He knows there's no reason to be offended by these kind and professionally maternal women: if they like you, it's from vocational bias.

After that, it's easy. I listen to him tell me all sorts of things I already know, he knows that I know them because I just told him I was the doctor's patient too, but he doesn't care. He tells me about his experience with the big zero, that's what he calls him, who swallowed his bullshit whole; what a sight the guy was, going all sympathetic and trying to catch him with gentleness when Tony respects only fists and cold steel.

The boy isn't used to having a friendly audience. He irritates me but I keep smiling and listening, and when he starts over on the same story for the third time, I interrupt him saying why don't we go to your place? He's startled, hesitates. Is going to refuse but changes his mind. I pay for our coffees, we walk to the métro station and take line 8 in the opposite direction from most commuters heading west to their office buildings. We get off at Montgallet, down in the southeast corner of Paris.

Tony still lives with his parents but they've left for work, and I learn that they're pharmacists. This surprises me because given his hangdog persona, I'd imagined his parents as drunks or incurably unemployed. Then I remember the facts I've read about crime, statistics in the newspapers showing that although parental maltreatment is more prevalent in the disadvantaged social classes, it can crop up anywhere.

Their home meets my expectations. The parquet floor in the hall is littered with pitfalls, craters between the loose slats and thickets of splinters at all the joints. I can see a living room and a master bedroom, furnished in mismatched functional things smacking of legacies from postwar houses in what were then modern suburbs. But you, where's your room? I ask Tony and he points down the hall to a door I'd assumed hid a closet. I set my lips in an expression of tender pity and observe you really don't get any breaks, do you.

Tony shoots me a nasty look then shrugs and leads me to the kitchen where he starts making coffee. I check out the sink with its reddish-brown crusts of crud and the shelves coated with greasy dust. Your parents, I remark, they don't seem to pay much attention to you, do they?

He clenches his fists; I twist the knife, adding it's obvious, one can see right away that you didn't get enough love, otherwise you'd never have done what you did in June outside the Lycée Paul-Valéry. The paper said poor girl, but right away I thought poor boy.

He drops the coffeepot that lands on the tiles like clashing cymbals

opens his fists

takes a step forward

I look at him

he looks at me

tensing up his silly-little-tough-guy muscles

he's so funny

he makes me laugh

so that I almost dislocate my jaw

then I've no idea what starts expanding inside me

I charge.

Lips on his trembling lips, impatience, edginess, bites, a swerve up to the ear, teeth attacking its outer shell, tongue against lobe, hands under the T-shirt, gooseflesh. Fingers that pinch, climb up the collar, grab the jawbone, and what a jawbone, so delicate, as if cut from crystal. Hand on the back of the neck, prey immobilized, completely pinned, tight grip. See what's

happening down below, if it's up, if it's sparking, gauge
its potential, adjust aim. Strong turbulence in seis-
mic zone. Flanking movement, pants in way, obstacle
belt, buckle-fumbling fingers, new obstacle arises. Obstacle promising. Hands on hands, beneath layers of
material, tips erect, redoubled vigor of obstacle. Pull-
overs tossed to floor, pants to follow, stuck on shoes,
get shoes off, uncertain movements, counterproduc-
tive haste, shoes stuck worse but getting there, getting
there. Majestic obstacle against white lace. Harpoon
obstacle, insert. Obstacle quivers, fights for survival.
But rout, retreat, useless struggle, enemy in flight,
victory too easy, absence of peril, triumph without
glory.* New strategy. Rekindle the battle. Hands every-
where, flying fingers, introduced, flicker turns to flame,
going to work, going to work. Another flop. Find something else. Imagination, imagination. On your knees,
Élisabeth. Open wide, back in business. Prey sighs,
relaxes, coasting along boulevard, gliding on alone.
Rabbit in tunnel, run over. Gets up, gets stuffed. Rabbit up in arms. Lasso, whoosh, obstacle under control.

---

* *À vaincre sans péril, on triomphe sans gloire.* (To vanquish without
peril brings a triumph without glory.) Pierre Corneille, *Le Cid*, act 2,
scene 2.—Trans.

Obstacle furious, roars, spends everything, spent. Obstacle drowsy.

So, says Tony, you came to wait for me in the Gare de l'Est just to do me a little favor.

We're lying on his parents' bed having a cigarette. Men's and women's clothes are strewn all around us. Ours are still lying on the kitchen floor.

I have a thing for tabloid news, I say without compromising myself.

Maybe, replies Tony with a trace of a smile, but you must not be getting nearly enough love. And since I wait for the follow-up he says at your age, I hope I won't still be consulting doctors, then he comes closer and I instinctively recoil.

What, he says with his naked savage smile, don't want to play anymore?

I'm out of bed in one bound but he follows me out of the bedroom, grabs my wrist and I realize I'm losing the match. I try to think but everything gets mixed up in my head and I can't figure out what attitude to adopt so I automatically defend myself, slapping him with my free hand. Tony lowers his head and rams into my stomach. I collapse against the wall, he comes on again, I straighten up and rain slaps on him that he deflects with his fists. When he grabs me by the forearms I drive my knee between his thighs then run toward the kitchen to get my things, but he catches me by the hair, tearing out a whole handful. I fall to the floor, dragging him down after me; we scratch each other with our nails, punch each other's bellies, and I close my eyes tightly, thrusting deep into his scrawny flesh while he grabs fistfuls of my skin, twisting and biting it. Crawling over the tiles, I steel myself against his blows as I concentrate on recovering a minimum of my clothing and getting out.

This takes perhaps ten or fifteen minutes. I give up everything I can. I let him take possession of this body that I inhabit so briefly and intermittently, and at the same time I collect my things behind my back while still only inching my way along to allay his suspicions. Finally we're at the foot of the front door, I no longer know what he's doing to me but I raise a hand toward the doorknob as if from underwater. Calling on my strength, benumbed during all those minutes that have drowned in a parallel dimension of my memory, I shove him violently back to get out onto the landing where he doesn't dare follow me. I dress hastily, run down the stairs. At two on the dot I ring the babysitter's doorbell.

13

A lovely three-bedroom with moldings and parquet floors, the apartment measures 915 square feet according to the prescriptions of the Carrez law determining effective usable surface area. The rooms branch off a central corridor enjoying an open view of a small paved square, southeast exposure. And if one were to lean out the window, braving the cold on this snowy Sunday, November 28—because it has been snowing for a week—one would see the Église Saint-Médard, surrounded by its tidy church garden. The net effect is charmingly postwar or opulently provincial.

You are not viewing the scene from outside the windows, however. Armed with a dainty watering can, you are refreshing the succulent plants that seem to thrive on a lack of regular care. No one is talking to them, or dusting them weekly with a soft moist cloth, and they keep growing. They must even be attached with adhesive tape to control their trajectories so that they stretch into the corners, toward the ceiling, along the interior stucco trim instead of overflowing their pots down to the carpet where they would blend into the design of vines and soon cover them up, vegetalizing the chevron-patterned parquet if you weren't taking them in hand.

Then the objects on the television and coffee table are cleansed of their dusty film. One of these bibelots slightly resembles that object on the doctor's bookshelves. This memory flits by you without pausing. You have no desire to meditate upon this relic, the history and provenance of which you know well. You also know the reason why it and not another knickknack sits there as a repository of special and arbitrary emotions, the legitimacy of which you do not challenge. You are sweeping.

Next you must open the bills, electricity, telephone, not the gas—cut off to economize and as a concession to reality. You check the columns of figures and put everything away in a trapezoidal writing desk. The clock says two thirty. Plenty of time left to vacuum the place before Julien arrives, which you do after closing the door to the middle room where the child is resting. At ten to three, you make a last tour of inspection, then go to stand at the window. He'll be late, a habit of his, and in the end he is remarkably punctual in his delays. You begin your vigil at three on the dot, however, preparing—almost hoping—to be disappointed, because then events will be following the course you have anticipated.

How handsome he was, Julien, and that hasn't changed since he left you. At three twenty, he appears in your launch window, creating an eclipse of memory: you imagine him coming toward you for the first time, naked, on offer, just as he presented himself three years earlier, free of all ties.

Your memory comes back. The breaches opened by the inevitable return to plodding reality, the pike staves that become lances, and you who couldn't see it coming because you were expecting a child and the horizon was bounded by the circumference of your belly. The suspicions wiped away with the dust when business meetings began to last forever. The phone calls made behind the bathroom door, the hurt you kept inside on every occasion, for example the cocktail party at Biron Concrete in June when the newly recruited Héloïse cruised dangerously close to Julien and you had to struggle to keep yourself from blasting her whenever she crossed your line of fire.

He's on the threshold of the apartment. He called up on the intercom and you buzzed him in. Standing perfectly still behind the door while he climbed up the three flights of stairs, you waited for him to ring and here he is in front of you. With locks of hair falling over his forehead. You could brush them back—after all, this man still belongs to you in the eyes of the law. You restrain your fingers just in time.

How are you he says while walking around you because you still haven't moved, and he goes into the living room to sit in the deepest armchair, the leather one. Hands crossed on your lap, you sit in a rather uncomfortable chair with a seat upholstered in a navy blue plaid. Julien gives a quick look around and exclaims these plants, good lord, it's monstrous, they're going to invade us all. You notice that he said us. But then he adds what are those marks on your arms, Viviane, they're awful. You roll your sleeves back down over your wrists now that you've finished cleaning and repeat meaningfully: invade us all, Julien? At first he doesn't understand. Then he does. Invade the hall, Viviane, I said invade the hall. You shrug as you announce I'm going to make some tea, you'll have some? Thanks he replies, which means yes or no, another habit of his.

While the kettle heats up in the kitchen, as you prepare a tray with two cups and watch the snow falling in the interior courtyard, you listen to the creaking of the parquet that tells you where your husband is. He seems to be roaming the living room, then advancing cautiously into the hall, gradually approaching the middle room. At last you hear the tiny squeak when he ventures a look inside at the sleeping child who is also his—it takes some effort to remember this but you concede the point.

The kettle whistles. Carrying in the tray you can see, through the now wide-open door, Julien bending over the baby. A wispy babbling reaches your ears. You study the teapot where the leaves are steeping. Not a very interesting sight but you often contemplate motionless things, waiting for them to reveal their secrets.

She seems to recognize me, he says in self-congratulation, plopping back into the armchair. Then he tries to talk about material arrangements, administrative procedures, rights and duties. What's going on outside the windows suddenly absorbs all your attention. You consider the movements on the square, the crowd at the tables under the heated outdoor umbrellas at the brasserie, the snow covering the central flower bed, pocked with footprints and the depredations of children.

Are you listening to me, Viviane?

Not really, Julien.

You have to be reasonable, Viviane.

I don't think so, Julien.

Then he invokes various responsibilities, and the welfare of the child. He knows you are a woman of good sense, you have always shown that despite differences of opinion, slight disagreements, and a few misunderstandings. For example, he goes on, it astonished me, that phone call from the police. I hadn't known you were seeing a doctor. That sort of thing, isn't it rather for people who are totally self-centered, don't you think?

I don't need you, you reply. What you take, you take away from me and I'm not going to make it any easier for you.

Julien murmurs God knows what in the direction of his lap but you would swear he said bitch. You exult in having managed so well to make him hate you now that love is gone. More tea? you ask, all smiles.

He shifts forward in the chair, sets his cup down on the tray, watches you pour the tea like a perfect hostess.

This isn't the right way, Viviane. The law is on my side. And anyway you can't manage all by yourself, you need help.

You stop serving the tea. The teapot tips toward the carpet and pours all the rest of its contents on the floor. When it's empty, you let go of it with a loud laugh. The carpet softens the fall but the china is fragile and shatters into pointed shards that fly into every corner of the room. On the other side of the wall, the child has begun to cry.

You have no idea, you say now, what I'm capable of.

Viviane, he tries, it's the stress, the emotional situation. You'll recover, you'll see things differently.

You reply fuck you and gather up everything on the tray, the cups, the saucers, the silver spoons, the sugar bowl, the milk jug, to throw it all at his face. He protects himself with his hands as he retreats, and you harry him all the way back to the front door. You expect him to beat it but he turns around one last time, looks you right in the eye and says it's not going to be this way, you'll see, I'm going to move into a new apartment with my new wife, we'll gain custody of the child, and you'll be left eating your heart out, then he clatters down the stairs while you stand paralyzed on the threshold.

14

Above the cradle, the lions and giraffes slow down and take off again, set in motion by a cord tied to the child's foot so that the slightest movement will bring the menagerie to life. For a good fifteen minutes now the baby has been trying to solve the mystery of causes and consequences. Left to yourself, you adjust the pleats in the curtains, wipe away some imaginary dust with the flat of your hand, pick up an object only to set it right down in the same place. Nightfall has finished blanketing the railway tracks, and the trains cutting across the window are stippled in white by the snow sweeping across the panes.

Your arms feel a little itchy. You roll up your sleeves, interrogating the long wounds running from the delta of veins at your wrists to vanish in the fold of the elbow and reappear at your neck. You try to recall how you got them but in truth you are seeking a more ancient element that has fallen into a deep well, leaving you with only a pale reflection.

You still retain a rather precise memory of your marriage. Back then every moment was a delight, and the doctor's wincing expression seemed to say poor thing, you're twenty years behind. Yes, you had almost forty years under your belt and the feeling of walking on water. You were unbearable. The slightest occurrence was a pretext for rhapsodizing about how loved you were, and how loving. The doctor was chafing in agony but you didn't give a hoot. He was paid to listen to you and was going to hear every detail. He was biding his time.

The problems began, in your opinion, three months after the wedding. That's an approximation; Julien would doubtless have a different idea. Today he would say from the beginning, from the beginning things were going wrong, I don't know how I ever let myself get involved in this business. So let's say—after three months. It started with your cat. Which wasn't strictly speaking yours, it belonged to your mother. You inherited it. You hadn't made a mystery of that last point. Neither had you made a big deal out of it. Raised in the Protestant ethic and the spirit of capitalism, you have a considerably reduced emotional range that you don't find at all inconvenient.

But Julien showed no interest in family affairs. It was enough for him to know that everyone was dead and he asked no questions, because they were all dead on his side as well, or just about. On the other hand, he was interested in the cat. From the kitchen to the bathroom, he found it constantly in his way and wanted to know when a new home might be found for it. He hadn't mentioned putting it down, he was still in love and there are things one leaves unsaid during those times when one fears ruffling another's feelings. He did mention dumping it in the woods, though. You plugged your ears and continued walking on water.

He kept at it. He said by the way, is that all you inherited? You replied no, there's also the apartment. He repeated the apartment? Real estate? What neighborhood? The 5th arrondissement you said. He smiled. (You might have told me sooner.) Then he wanted to see for himself and you agreed, to have some peace. Leaving your mother's apartment he'd estimated its market value and announced that the furniture wouldn't bring much but every little bit helps. You'd suggested a walk in the Jardin des Plantes.

At the entrance to the rain forest greenhouse he'd asked when you were thinking of putting it on the market. You'd scraped a bit of gravel in the path with the tip of your shoe and made embarrassed faces. Finally you'd said I'd rather not sell, we don't need the money, we make a good living, let's forget it. He then asked how long you had been holding on to this apartment. You took ten euros out of your wallet to pay for the greenhouse tickets. He asked again in front of the prickly pear cactus. Suddenly you felt very hot. You took off your jacket and fumbled in your purse for a tissue, hoping to take as long as possible. When you looked up, Julien had moved off toward the palmetto palm. You took a little stroll, patting your cheeks, then joined him near the orchids. He'd asked the question again. You'd answered to get him off your back. Seven years? Eight? He'd said Viviane, there's something really wrong here.

In the cradle the child has set out to break her toy, tired of these stupid animals that go around in circles without ever leaving their orbit. Great thrashings of the lower limbs communicate their contradictory injunctions to the mobile, sending lions and giraffes flying in every direction, crashing together like clacking castanets. You're about to take her in your arms when the doorbell rings. It's nearly midnight. No one has yet visited you in this apartment and you wonder who it could possibly be.

Well it's the police.

In the doorway stands that inspector from the other day, that Philippot with the tender, inviting eye, who were he to go about it more skillfully would wangle out any and all confessions. He is accompanied by a subordinate but you don't register any details of his physiognomy. You look the inspector up and down, waiting for an explanation and he offers none, showing you his police credentials according to regulations and saying Madame Hermant, you're to come with us, collect the child's things and please come along.

What does one do in these circumstances. One flutters in vain, asking questions nobody answers. The policemen hurry you along, put things into your hands barking you'll be needing this and that and in the end they hand you a travel bag they've found in a packing box and you stuff your daughter's things inside it. Plucking the cradle from its frame, they carry it out to the stairs and you run after them, dashing down the steps behind the child they're carrying off, tripping over the coat dangling from your arms, your shoes only halfway on your feet.

A vehicle is parked outside the building. Its door is open; a policeman motions you inside while the officer who's carrying the cradle and the traveling bag hands them over to a man who has come out of the shadows. It's Julien. He's there, he doesn't look at you, he grabs the loot and disappears. You're given no time to take in this picture. The policemen push you into the backseat where you find yourself between the inspector and his subordinate. The driver pulls away immediately and you look desperately into the rearview mirror, pleading for a sign, an augury, some hope, but the face in the mirror does not recognize you.

15

Let's see where we are, says the chief inspector. On the other side of the desk, the prisoner is slumped in defeat. We received a phone call from your husband, he continues; it seems that you are not yourself these days. So tell me, what are those marks on your arms, Madame Hermant?

The woman's arms are covered; she studies them without moving. Then the chief inspector explodes: he stands up, pounding his fat fist on the desk, and walks around it yelling stop fucking with me, show me your arms now and tell me how they got that way.

Since she still does nothing, the inspector who brought her in steps forward and pulls up one sleeve of her sweater. The chief inspector is right next to her, the mass of his face swollen in a grotesque close-up. All she sees is an orbit, black against the backlighting because it's the accused who is illuminated, the lamp shining in her face, the face of an animal dragged from the depths of its burrow. But in that instant she loses all fear. A feeling of destiny sweeps over her: she awaits the fatal blow.

You've been fighting? bellows the chief inspector, his thick breath shooting directly into the nostrils of the accused woman, you had a fight and the other one fought back, is that it? You look like a middle-class lady but you have your little moods, get angry and then you can't answer for yourself? Huh, Madame Hermant?

The echo of these suppositions dies away in the office, and she says yes looking down at her lap, yes I had a fight. And who with? continues the chief inspector in the same vein, the syllables falling like projectiles around the person in pain. With the Boujon kid, she admits at last, I fought with Tony Boujon.

The two men draw back smartly. What the hell were you doing with him? demands the chief inspector. So then comes the admission that she'd undertaken some research. Cut out newspaper articles. Waited for him in the Gare de l'Est to talk to him but regrets that now, it wasn't a good idea in the end. Then she falls silent once more. After which neither the shouting of the chief inspector nor that of the inspector when they switch roles (counting on the contrast to soften up the target) nor their kicks at the chair she clings to until she finally lets go and winds up on the floor—nothing will rouse her from the mutism into which she has withdrawn, and they lock her up out of spite.

The cell is about six feet deep by four and a half wide. Provided with a cot and a door of safety glass, it is absolutely clean. The walls do not weep with humidity; no insect scoots around the tile floor. If one wishes to go to the toilet, permission is granted; one is accompanied by an officer of one's own sex. One can also obtain a glass of water but nothing to eat. At last the possibility of a phone call is offered. The person in question ignores this offer. She curls up on the cot with her palms over her eyelids to make everything black, because that's still where one sees the best.

This will give you time, the chief inspector said before tossing her in the hole, to think about the consequences of your actions. Well that's just what she wants, to bring some order to her memory. Instead of coming to light, however, events are retreating ever deeper into darkness.

Bereft of her recent past, she shelters in ancient history. She remembers the mother who has no more beginning than end, impossible to date by any method, introspection or carbon 14. And next to the monolith appears a tiny shadow. A personage who was loved after a fashion, with what remained of affection, but who then simply evaporated one fine day: they were no longer three in the apartment on Place Saint-Médard, they were two, face-to-face like two porcelain figures. And if the disappearance of the third element upset the equilibrium of the landscape for a while, it was quickly relegated to the status of remembrance, like those bibelots on the mantelpiece one polishes automatically but would never give up for anything in the world, so indispensible are they to the new configuration of the whole. Explanations were doubtless demanded, around the age of twelve or fourteen, when one hopes through skillful inquiry to obtain justice and amends. It quickly becomes clear, however, that an absence of cause is better than a slew of unsatisfactory motives, and silence reclaims its due.

The person on the cot sways from right to left and vice versa. Time passes and might flow on forever, but a back twinge or a tiny ache in one knee finally brings the body back to mind. Leading to a lifting of the head, a change

of position. An examination of what's going on outside, beyond the glass door, in the corridor where a few
scarce officers pass without ever looking at the prisoner.

Toward the middle of the night, they remove her
from her cage to return her to the same office. Another
guest is already seated in one of the visitors' chairs.

Sit down, Madame Hermant, orders the chief inspector. You will now tell me how the two of you met.

That's her, Tony Boujon insists loudly, she's the one
that came up to me, then she wanted to go to my place,
it's her that planned it all!

Well, Madame Hermant, what do you say to that?

It's true, says the humiliated woman. I saw his photo
in the paper. I don't know why I got the idea to follow
him but I did and I regret it.

The story of this episode must be told. Everything
must be gone over in extreme detail, the approach, the
assault, the tangled limbs, and precisely how it went, in-
cluding what fluids were exchanged, until the suspects
agree on a common version. Which doesn't present major difficulties, since the boy wants to downplay his
guilt and the woman wants to comply. She says yes, it's
true, I threw myself at him then I don't know what came
over me, I scratched him, I bit him, he defended himself

as best he could, and the boy enthusiastically endorses that version, repeating yes, that's it, that's totally what happened, she wouldn't let go of me, I didn't know how to get her off me. The policemen take down this version. Sometimes they look up, having trouble believing that two suspects would agree so zealously with each other. But in the other business, the important one, with the doctor, Tony Boujon has a cast-iron alibi. He is careful to bring this up, how he had to go to work earlier that day, a machine had broken down, they'd called him in to help out and three workmen can testify that he was there all night.

Then perhaps Madame Hermant is your accomplice, suggests the chief inspector; perhaps she is the hand and you the brains in this case. Everyone in the room looks at everyone else, considering this hypothesis, each one weighing it individually, and it's so idiotic that in order to save face the chief inspector is the first to abandon it, rising and swatting the kid, who lands on the floor as the fat man leaves the office saying little bastard.

The two accused don't dare turn around to see if the inspector is still behind them. Tony climbs painfully back onto his chair and they wait in perfect submission. Finally they figure out that they're alone but still don't move, staying on their chairs for long minutes that become hours. Shortly after dawn, an officer frees him and takes her back to her hole.

A few more hours pass during which she ties her hair in knots, rocking back and forth this time, hypnotized by her own movement. An officer enters the cell to place a glass of water next to her and asks if she wants to go with her to the toilet. She replies no thank you. At the end of the afternoon, someone opens the door again to tell her she is free.

She works her way slowly out of the cell, and hugging the walls so harshly illuminated by the ceiling light in the corridor, blinking and lightly touching these walls in case she has to lean on one, she reaches the elevator, crosses the lobby of the police station and finds herself outside. At first she can't remember very well how to get home, what would be the best bus or métro line. She remembers that her arms are empty and that the child who belongs there is missing.

16

In your lap you're rocking the case of knives you just retrieved from your husband's apartment. This time you did not run into Madame Urdapilla. The apartment had not changed much since the other day, except that things belonging to the absent baby were lying around the second bedroom. You called Julien after leaving his place. Naturally you did not say where you were. You said I've been thinking: I got carried away the other day, we do have to get organized about the baby, adding I'm going to sell my mother's apartment so do you want to meet with me late this afternoon to talk about things? Julien said okay. A week has gone by and Julien now understands what it's like taking care of a child. He would be only too happy to get rid of her for a few days.

Outside the window, the snow still blankets the gravel of the railway beds and the sky looks like a sea of cotton. You stop the rocking chair, shove the knives into your purse, and leave.

The ruins of Arènes de Lutèce lie about five hundred yards from Place Saint-Médard in the Latin Quarter. You go through the gates and along the path by what remains of the Gallo-Roman amphitheater, then climb the stepped terraces to look down into the arena. Buildings of middling height close the perimeter to the north. To the south are trees, a thick wall of snowcapped branches shutting out the city. Perched atop the tiers, you see the gates through which were released the hungry lions, and through the stage door appears your mother.

She spots you right away, a large shape swaddled in your gray coat like a makeshift tent. When she reaches you she says aren't you a little crazy, in this weather, you could have come to my place, after all. You reply I know, but I'm in a hurry. You observe the texture of her image. The extreme materiality of the features that are just as you've always known them, the bumps, the hollows, the special glow of the skin, the general allure like no other. You are really crazy she says again indulgently, and looks as if she's about to reach toward you, but in the end she holds back, turns, and vanishes among the trees. You remain alone with the knives, delivered up to the snow that begins falling again.

Julien will arrive from the northeast. Getting off the No. 86 bus in front of the Institut du Monde Arabe, he'll walk past the Faculté des Sciences, slalom among the poorly parked vehicles and the perpetual work in progress along that stretch of the sidewalk, then at the intersection with Rue des Écoles, take Rue Linné toward the Jardin des Plantes. After the small supermarket, he'll turn onto Rue des Arènes to reach Rue Monge.

With your back to the arena, you walk toward the circular barred fence that surrounds the enclosure, following the curve of the street. There is one place, at the junction with Rue de Navarre, where one can observe the path of an eventual passerby—because for the moment there are none—from Rue Linné to Rue Monge. You are standing at that spot. Across the street are apartment buildings of noble discretion, stylish without excessive complications. Now and then a window opens to allow the shaking out of a tablecloth. A shadow passes a curtain; a cat behind a window demands the opening of his aquarium but by the time someone complies it's too late, he has lost interest.

After half an hour you can definitely see your

husband down the street. Julien seems to be carrying the world on his shoulders, which for an instant you again see naked against yours, enveloping you to perfection. You drive away that image. You replace it with the one of everything he owes you, the knives in your purse, your flyaway daughter, your runaway mother. You draw close to the barred fence but of course he doesn't see you. Muffled by the snow, silent, invisible, you run toward the exit of the amphitheater and by the time you reach the sidewalk, he's already turning onto Rue Monge. It's too late to call to him discreetly, to lead him over to the métro entrance no one ever uses because it has a hundred steps whereas the main entrance over on Place Monge has an escalator.

Julien is striding along but you have no trouble matching his fleeing pace. Nothing happens along the way to Place Saint-Médard, where you're careful to stay back, skirting the church garden while he's busy with the keypad lock a few yards ahead of you. He vanishes into your mother's building—the one that was yours as well for twenty-eight years, yes, that's how long you lived there, but no one forced you to stay, you liked the place.

On the square there is a brasserie where the first

floor offers an excellent view of the surrounding neighborhood. You choose a table near the window and order
a hot toddy, never taking your eyes off the door through
which Julien has disappeared, where he reappears a few
minutes later, only to stop at the intercom. He taps on
his cell phone and correlatively yours begins to vibrate
in your pocket. You observe that three messages have
already been recorded. You do not open the phone; you
do not listen to the messages. The object continues to
vibrate on the table and Julien's name appears on the
screen, calling and calling again in the void.

Then he walks around the square, enters the bookstore. Your husband strolls among the tables of new arrivals, picking up and immediately putting back books,
checking the titles lined up on the shelves without in all
likelihood remembering any of them, finally leaving the
store to use his phone but you still don't answer. You
order a second hot toddy.

Julien enters the bookstore again. This time he goes
to the back, chooses something from a rack of graphic
novels, and methodically turns the pages until the end.
When he has finished the book he comes out again
and night is falling on the square. Julien makes one last
call but this time your phone doesn't vibrate, and the

person he's now calling seems more approachable because he's talking on the phone—you can clearly see his lips move, quickly then slowing down as the conversation progresses—until having definitively given up on you, he retraces his steps and leaves the square.

Is it the effect of that soppy expression on your husband's face or the toddies multiplying as you found the time dragging?—anyway your balance isn't as solidly grounded as before. You start tailing him again, preparing to hail him and lead him over to that lonely métro entrance you'd thought of earlier, in the rocking chair, as a suitable sign-off place for your crime. But now Julien is walking right past Rue des Arènes. He's leading you toward another neighborhood you know well, Rue des Carmes and its police station. Your husband is walking some fifteen yards ahead of you, passing the florist's, the hardware store, the wine shop, the bakery you pass in turn without hearing the name called out behind you.

Nor do you recognize the voice of Gabrielle, the doctor's wife who, having just completed a little inventory at the Rue du Pot-de-Fer apartment, had been on her way back to the one she shares with her lover. Refusing to hear this name chasing after you, it's impossible for you to know that she's right on your heels, hopping in the snow, grabbing her cell and calling Inspector Philippot, then Angèle, to whom the police have recently introduced her. In the end, the two of them didn't hit it off too badly, sharing as they do many experiences and opinions regarding the deceased.

So Gabrielle verifies some of the givens in the problem and resumes trotting several paces behind you, as you pursue your husband through cobblestoned streets where tourists buy souvenirs of Notre Dame and where he at last stops short, as if undecided. Fearing he might spot you, you duck into an entrance to a movie theater where you don't spot Gabrielle, who has taken refuge there a moment earlier through the other entrance for the same reason. No, you don't see anything around you, too preoccupied by the form you are shadowing ahead of you, which soon sets off through the crowd.

You rush after him, the widow tagging along. She's becoming less and less cautious in her pursuit: glued to her phone, she's now transmitting geographic coordinates, precisely following your movements. At last Julien enters a jewelry store, comes out again carrying a pretty package. You'd love to tear it from his hands but with an effort you breathe in, breathe out. It's painful for air to circulate through your lungs compressed by nervous tension and that slight nausea you've been experiencing constantly since a little while ago. You keep following him, though, on to the Seine where you're soon crossing the Saint-Michel bridge.

Which leads to the Île de la Cité, police headquarters, the Palais de Justice. To the Conciergerie and its towers of evil memory: cold jails, final judgments, gleaming guillotines. You carry the icy weight of those stone walls on your drooping shoulders as you press on through the snow. But your steps begin to falter on their own and you think that if Julien were to turn around in that instant, the black water beneath the bridge would become the only way out. Perhaps it's this image that heightens your nausea as you reach the island. Or hunger. You think back to your last meal. It was the day before, and besides, just two small tins of sardines eaten straight from the can, they don't really count. That's bad, alcohol on an empty stomach, anyone could tell you so.

Then Julien slows down as well, looking around, seeking something or someone. And in fact there does seem to be a feminine form at the corner of police headquarters. Your husband hesitates long enough to confirm that this is indeed the person he's been hurrying to join; his pace quickens as he heads for the woman who now moves away from the wall to meet him, and it just so happens to be Héloïse. Your stomach heaves.

And again that name is called out behind you. You pretend you don't hear, but it keeps coming back, three, ten, twenty times, the astonishment growing with each call, as if this name had to be endlessly repeated to make sure that it is indeed you at the end of the bridge, Élisabeth.

Veiled by the snow clinging to your lashes, your eyelids open with difficulty, but you still recognize Angèle arriving to your right. In a panic, you whip around only to run into Gabrielle and the inspector with his subordinate, closing on you fast while Julien and Héloïse finally notice your presence and he says Viviane, Viviane, what are you doing here?

You need to react, to fight, but suddenly something much more urgent happens. No matter how hard you concentrate, how deeply you breathe, air is no longer reaching your lungs. Declining to be sucked in, it simply ebbs away. You find it provoking that the mechanism is breaking down like this. You devote all your energy to forcing stubborn air into your pharynx but in vain, and you cannot remember having ever experienced anything this unpleasant. You look in supplication toward your husband but can no longer see him, then toward the inspector but cannot find him, either. You glimpse only car headlights on the ground and streetlights in the sky, which quickly meld together. You no longer know which is which, where up is or down, if it's yourself out here, someone else, or if it's simply a dream—or if you'll ever wake up. You stop breathing altogether. You fall.

17

They take you to the oldest hospital in Paris, the Hôtel-Dieu, a stone's throw from the Palais de Justice. Your first days there go so badly that they ply you with pills, like the ones the doctor used to prescribe for you only much more effective ones. Soon you are basically a vegetable. Staring at the walls absorbs all your attention. You never tire of studying the variations in their angles when you tip your head to the right, the left, up, then down. A large smile graces your countenance; a dribble of saliva escapes your lips. It takes you several minutes to notice this, and another few to consider taking action, deciding whether it's all right to let it run down to your chin. Sometimes you correct the situation with aquatic languor; sometimes you don't give a damn.

Now and then someone in a white coat appears to evaluate your condition, eventually wipe off your lips, and give you your medicine. After a few days (you'd be hard put to say how many) they decide to try diminishing the dosage, see how that works. Very bad idea. As soon as the last round has worn off, you're so beside yourself that you frighten the chief physician, who says get her back on meds, she's not ready, not by a long shot. The inspector cooling his heels outside in the corridor goes back to the police station.

Still, in due course your body gets used to these substances circulating through your arteries, visiting your synapses to numb them nicely. A few objects now stand out from the walls. Which won't get you very far because once anything sharp, pointed, or blunt has been eliminated, not much remains to provide entertainment. That leaves a bedside table on wheels with some plastic cups. They are empty. If there was any water in them, you drank it, but you don't remember that or anything else. Wait, your daughter. You rather think that you have a daughter. Which then means that you also have a mother. You do remember those two.

You notice that you're wearing some very uncomfortable pajamas, of an indeterminate material between cloth and paper. And the sheets on your bed—very strange, these sheets. They seem like plastic. At any rate, they're impossible to rip up. You're also beginning to hear noise out in the corridor, brief exchanges between the hospital personnel and the police, the examining magistrates and the lawyers, interspersed with loony ululations followed by long silences. That's it, you get the picture.

Then one morning, suddenly, you see things quite clearly. You are also quite scared. When the nurse brings breakfast—four pieces of melba toast with a bowl of brown liquid supposed to be tea—you sit on the edge of your bed and say calmly that this cannot continue, I do not want to stay here, and you have to give me back my child. The nurse studies you inscrutably and goes to inform the chief physician.

A large square person with a reddish-brown mustache, the latter questions you without listening to the answers, observing your reactions. When you say that you are scared, he says that isn't important. You say yes it is, I'm really very scared, you have to do something, prescribe me some other pills, I can give you their names, I have to have them or I'll go crazy. He replies you're not in a supermarket and leaves.

Left alone with your fear, you sweat profusely. The pajamas stick to your limbs. Soon your breathing goes awry the way it did the other day on the Saint-Michel bridge; thousands of flies take off inside your skull, hammering your ears, and your strength abruptly returns. You raise a fist against the reinforced door, on which you pound, hitting until your arm turns blue with bruising, until the pain moves from your head into your body and they come and give you your pills.

That lasts another three days; then they must have set up something with the inspector because as soon as the antipsychotics wear off, he turns up with his subordinate, the one whose face you can never remember. You demand a lawyer. The inspector says listen, Madame Hermant, we're not in a movie, this isn't how it works in real life, you have to answer some questions first. He then lets you stew until the cows come home, asking easy questions to keep from being bored, along the lines of tell me what happened back there on the Saint-Michel bridge. But it's easy to see he doesn't care, he's just waiting for you to go off your nut while he watches and the subordinate picks his teeth with his nails.

After an hour you're ready for anything and it all comes out, but the story is so confused that he asks you to slow down, try to be more specific with the chronology, Madame Hermant, because all this isn't really very clear. Gradually your narrative builds up, and you recount in detail your day on November 15. How you got the knives from your husband's apartment, made an appointment with the doctor and left the child to the care of no one while you went to Rue de la Clef. How the doctor provoked that inexplicable explosive reaction in you. How you committed that act you ought never to have carried out—just look at how your mother brought you up, a model of perfection.

After which the inspector requires more details. The circumstances must be solidly established, it's important, he says, for the dossier. The subordinate is taking notes at quite a clip, you provide all the details the inspector wants but he keeps asking for more and gets on your nerves in the end. You have admitted your crime, what else does he want, it's as if he doesn't believe you. Finally the subordinate's wrist gives out, so they call it a day. You say okay, can I have my pills now? And the inspector says I'll see what I can do.

Then the specialists parade through to examine you, putting you through certain tests that seem simple enough at first, where you must solve problems to demonstrate the logic of your thinking, the depth of your reasoning. They don't reveal their conclusions but you can guess from their faces that they've seen better, they've seen worse.

Next they send you the chief evaluator, and this woman wants to see how you think, how your recent ordeals have affected your belief system and psychological defenses. She seems particularly interested in your mother. Yes, tell her about your mother. No problem. You talk about the apartment and everything else: the furniture, the knickknacks on the mantelpiece, the ivy in the living room, the floral design in the carpet. She observes you thoughtfully.

The days go by; you have no idea whether the court-ordered appraisal is really moving forward but you no longer think about the future. In any case you will not be staying on at the Hôtel-Dieu, which is not a place for long-term care. The feeling is something like traveling on a train or cruising in the Mediterranean: time seems suspended. Satisfied with your recent composure, the chief physician reduces your medications. And it appears that this hospitalization has in fact calmed you down.

On the other hand, you're now becoming seriously bored. You complain to the nurse, the one who does not include empathy among her main attributes. Still, she hasn't the heart to refuse you a little distraction and hands you a tabloid magazine full of divorces and eating disorders. You sympathize. Seeing you touched by these troubles that doubtless move her as well, she allows you a pencil to play the games. You fill in the blanks, erase the answers with the end of the pencil, then start over again the next morning. After a few days, you have more or less memorized the solutions and erased lots of holes through the pages.

The inspector comes to see you at the end of the week. He requires two or three more details regarding November 15, which you wearily supply. No, you do not have a chronometer, you would really like to help him out but there are things that escape even their supposed author. Fine, we'll leave it at that, he says and presents some papers for signature. You sign without knowing what you're signing and you couldn't care less.

After another week, you are so well behaved that they give you back your daughter. She arrives with her baby gear, the cradle, the mobile, extra outfits, and pulls the usual stunt: carried in screaming, she shuts up as soon as you take her from the nurse's arms. The reunion is heartwarming. So much so that it distracts you a bit more from your problems with the law. On that count, they're still not telling you anything. The specialists visit you now and again but interest in your case seems on the wane. Soon they stop giving you any meds during the day, only a tablet at night to help you sleep.

18

Pascal Planche.

Pascal Planche owns three dust-colored suits. The first of flannel for summer wear, the second in a wool mixture for winter, the last of synthetic material for other eventualities (stains, delayed dry cleaning, torrents of rain). His shirts feature stripes in a matching color, or sometimes a small check. His shoes belong to no identifiable species: moccasins, Oxfords, bucks, sneakers, loafers, or flip-flops. He loves them, though, spends his Sundays taking care of them. After lining the pairs up in front of him, he gets out the shoeshine box where he keeps his supplies. On one side, rags and sponges; on the other, polishes and creams. Pascal spreads out a piece of newspaper on the floor and gets to work. He proceeds by stages rather than by pairs, judging that this method is more relaxing. One shoe after the other, he buffs off dirt with a soft, long-bristled brush, then massages the leather with an enriching liquid, brushes again, shines, waxes, polishes, rubs, until the process is complete and he enjoys an invariable and well-earned satisfaction.

Pascal lives on Rue de l'Argonne in the 19th arrondissement, by the Corentin-Cariou métro station. On Monday mornings he takes the 7 line to the Archives Nationales, where he is in charge of the department preserving draft contracts written by Parisian notaries. Overlooking the beautiful main courtyard, his office is a cramped room of about one hundred square feet, and in his domain boxes are stacked floor to ceiling, carefully labeled. He can find any document without a moment's hesitation: his system is perfectly organized, without any possibility of failure or mistake.

Pascal is very obliging. He helps out his colleagues when they're inundated with work, carries groceries for old ladies, waters plants for people on vacation, feeds the cats. And he's easy to get along with, his friends would add, army vets who get together every Friday evening: Planche is always up for everything, a few drinks, going to a movie or helping someone move, supporting any soccer team if that will please someone.

He's so obliging that they never know what he really thinks. In fact they've ended by believing he doesn't think anything.

As a result, Pascal has been on medication for seven and a half years: two tablets morning and evening, plus another whenever his brain gets ready to blow out the valve in his skull. At least that's the expression noted down by the doctor during his first consultation. Ever since, Pascal had had the Monday 10:30 appointment. On Mondays he used to show up at the Archives at 8:30, then swiped out again at 10:10 to go see his physical therapist, he told his colleagues. That a man in his profession should have back problems seems quite plausible. So off he would go, taking the 7 once more to Censier-Daubenton. By 11:20 he'd be back, and would finish work at 5:40 to make up for the seventy minutes spent dealing with his pain. Still, there was some worry about the fact that his condition never seemed to improve. Chronic, it's now chronic, Planche would reply evasively, then resume filing his documents.

Torn between the shame of informing and his duty as a citizen, it was Planche as well who told police about the telephone conversation on November 15 between

Viviane Hermant and the doctor concerning the appointment made for around, and I mean around, the
time of the murder. Planche's name appears for the first
time in *Le Parisien* on Wednesday, December 22, a paper the nurse will hand to Viviane the following day.
Well, according to that edition and with regard to that
same November 15, Planche was not able to account for
his actions between 5:40 and 9:00 that evening. Worse,
having told the police that he'd gone straight home from
work as he did every day, he'd found himself contra-
dicted by his next-door neighbor.

In that horseshoe-shaped apartment building on
Rue de l'Argonne, the windows of the neighbor woman
give onto Pascal's living room and bedroom. And they
were dark until 8:35. She remembers that well because
that is the unusually late hour at which he arrived home
that evening, just when the final episode of a quiz show
celebrating a certain trivial conception of general cul-
ture was due to begin. She never misses the concluding
episodes: the TV host is so handsome and he's on for a
longer time at the end of the series. And so Pascal finds
himself in police custody (*Le Parisien*, December 25).
Merry Christmas, says the nurse to Viviane.

Several days follow during which nothing happens.

Then one morning, the door to her cell is left open. Viviane has no particular intention of escaping, but it's been some time since she's had a breath of fresh air. Hugging the baby to her shoulder, she ventures out into the corridor where two nurses are pushing rolling carts loaded with medical instruments. To the right, a white wall breached by dozens of cells; to the left, a series of sturdily barred windows overlooking a bare and narrow courtyard. She makes it to the elevator and, since the nurses aren't paying any attention to her, steps into the car. The doors close, reflecting on their panels the image of a rather pale woman with very messy hair. Aiming at random, she pushes another button.

It's exactly the same configuration on that floor, except that there aren't any bars on the windows and there are signs at the beginning of the corridor indicating the direction to various wards. She starts down the corridor and winds up taking a tour that brings her back to the elevator, which she takes to the ground floor this time. Here the décor is completely different. Staying close to the arched windows opening onto an interior courtyard bounded by a labyrinth of evergreen shrubs and a kind of Greek temple, Viviane follows a gallery all the way down to the reception area. In the vast lobby where the two galleries framing the courtyard come together, patients sit drowsing in metal chairs, shuffling their social security papers while awaiting their turn, and right in the center of the far wall is the entrance. Or the exit, as you please. Perfectly accessible, simply a matter of heading toward it to trigger the automatic doors and go out into the open air.

A cloud of dust overwhelms your brain. Stimulates your sudatory system, sends tremors through your fingers. On the verge of vertigo, you cling to the child to save yourself from falling. The baby pulls you through. Steady as you go, you beat a retreat and five minutes later, you're back in your cell, sitting demurely on the hospital bed. You are waiting for today's lunch: scalloped chicken and kohlrabi purée.

19

On January 4 your husband shows up. Julien Hermant, yes, that is his name, he's out in the corridor and the nurse wants to know if she can allow him in, or if that might upset you (he's the one asking, I'm just passing it along). You agree to see him and, without responding to his embarrassed greetings, immediately press for news about Pascal Planche.

Locked up, they've locked him up, exclaims the still-astonished Julien, who has brought along some magazines and asks timidly if he might hold the child. You know, he continues after she's handed over, I thought it would be a good idea to relieve you somewhat of this responsibility, but I quickly realized that at this age, a child needs her mother, and I preferred to give her back to you, given that the doctors said things were looking up. Because they are looking up, right? he concludes hopefully.

The next visit is from Gabrielle. She considers you without any particular animosity, perched on the edge of her chair like a statue unable to find an acceptable plinth. You murmur something in the way of apologies but the widow waves them away. She has come to wrap things up. To continue the story of her life, since you find it so interesting.

Gabrielle discovered that she was rich. Not worth millions, of course, but enough to keep her going for a while. And suddenly she realized that she didn't need anyone. She packed up, moved back to the Rue du Pot-de-Fer apartment, threw out the doctor's crummy watercolors and settled in. Angèle's baby was born without incident, and although the obstetrician had sworn the contrary, it was a boy. At the time the mother hadn't come up with a given name, but we ended by agreeing on Achille, confides the widow. Oh yes, she adds, having almost forgotten, I also had dinner with your husband. He certainly is handsome. But lord, is that man uptight. Well, what time is it—twenty past noon, I have to go now. See you around sometime, Viviane.

No more visits after that. So, you take a few walks. You explore the hospital, the main courtyard framed by three stories of galleries, the top one of which offers a lofty view over the parvis of Notre Dame. Tourists enclosed behind a fence on the cathedral roof peer out at the panorama. Sometimes they wave and you wave back.

One morning, out of curiosity, you go to the chapel off the passage linking the upper galleries. A big disappointment, not at all worthy of the first-rate establishment where you're staying. The chapel is a tiny plywood room slapped together in the 1970s with two rows of mismatched chairs and a no-frills altar beneath a run-of-the-mill stained glass window. Actually, it reminds you of the domed Central Committee Chamber at the Paris headquarters of the Communist Party—not that you have a revolutionary past, but Julien used to love dragging you off to that Oscar Niemeyer cupola on Place du Colonel-Fabien so that he could rave about its architectural beauty. You don't linger in the chapel.

On January 10 the chief physician arrives with his entourage. He examines you for two minutes, says everything's fine to no one in particular, you can take her to the nurse. Who tells you to hurry and gather up your belongings. You collect the things that have accumulated in the cell as the weeks have gone by and cram them into big plastic bags. Carrying the baby, you follow the nurse along the corridor, into the elevator, down to the ground floor gallery. The nurse escorts you to the exit: tripping the automatic doors, she delivers you and your bags to the sidewalk, where a dark gray taxi awaits. In the backseat, your mother is quietly smoking a cigarette.

20

It is a city fortified with concrete through and through. It could be Saint-Nazaire, Cherbourg, Le Havre. Rows of buildings thrown up in haste after the Liberation form a rampart against the water, all traces of bombardment carefully removed. Along the base of the façades snake the floating docks of the marina, the asphalt road, the shingle beach. The sea and the overcast sky roll toward each other with the speed of an outboard, and at the far end the pale sun sinks into the water.

You are leaning on your elbows at the balustrade of a terrace on the ninth floor. All the apartment windows have full western exposure onto the open water plied by ferries, oil tankers, container ships. To the south rise the cranes of the industrial port, looming over the deserted wharf like long-suffering pterodactyls. Then

come the domes of the refinery and the vertical labyrinth of a cemetery.

The apartment comprises three rather well-laid-out
rooms, with the bedrooms on either side of the living
room, plus the bathroom and toilet together at the end
of the hall. The interior decoration is minimal but the
packing boxes are gone. All your belongings have been
put away in cupboards and closets and on newly installed shelves, an operation requiring numerous trips to
major hardware stores. You didn't do anything. Catalogs
were brought to you, you checked off the models, left the
details to the professionals. You got out your checkbook.

So you left the Hôtel-Dieu, and your mother brought
you home. In the weeks that followed you slept a great
deal. Sometimes you watched afternoon television,
where airy and insubstantial things happen in faraway
settings. Surgeons two-time their wives with nurses
pregnant by airline pilots, the husbands die through
mishaps with ice picks, and the widows drive convert-
ibles against a backdrop of azure blue. They all lulled
you like the memory of an old joke.

In March, you were already feeling more ener-
getic: it was time to look to the future. Well, Biron

Concrete was—how to put this—none too eager to see you again. Jean-Paul did not come right out and say no, Viviane, I'd prefer that you not return to your old job, or I would like Héloïse to replace you. He said you know, I have contacts—partners, entrepreneurs, district organizations—adding, do you know Normandy? Can you imagine, they're looking for an assistant regional director of communications, so I thought, hold on, why not you. Wouldn't you like a little change of air?

You took a train at the Gare Saint-Lazare, interviewed for the job for appearance's sake. Two weeks later, all taken care of: the salary level, notice given for the Rue Cail apartment, a new place on the waterfront (your only requirement). You started work in your new position on April 15. It's a job, no more, no less. You go every day to an office, where you do what is asked of you and leave at six o'clock.

The local child-care woman, in your opinion, can't hold a candle to the old one. She talks a lot, asks too many questions, never waits for the answers before asking new ones. The advantage is you can let her babble on surrounded by screaming children, whereas yours is so well behaved that at times she frightens you.

You did not bring along the rocking chair. That is

not where you read the press clippings collected during your stay at the Hôtel-Dieu, nor is it where you knit while you go over the thread of events. You do all that in bed, before setting aside your knitting to apply your hands to a different, more relaxing activity.

And so, after your little panic attack on November 15, you did indeed make an appointment with the doctor for the end of the afternoon, and you showed up right on time. But you were not alone. You were with your daughter, whom you were not going to leave on her own at the age of twelve weeks, after all. What a face the doctor made: he was even more huffy with you than usual, yawning as he listened to you and renewed your prescription.

After which everything becomes very strange, as if someone else's memories had been instilled in you. Yet you know they are true. You leave the office. Once more, you have not gotten what you wanted. You think, this is a waste of time, there's no point, it just keeps me on the hook, that's all. Dusk seeps into the stairwell; a potted plant watches over the silence. You sit down on the top step, curved like a parasol over the baby. You cry.

Someone else is already in the office. You heard the

bell ring when you were with the doctor and he let in the next patient using a switch on the low table near his armchair. The person entered the waiting room, closing the door to the landing. When that patient leaves the office, perhaps a quarter of an hour later, you are still sitting on the top step but your tears have dried. You look up when he passes you to dash outside. It's a momentary exchange of glances, a high-angle/low-angle shot in which you both seem equally distraught. He makes as if to do something, sees the baby asleep against you. Runs away. You have no memory of his face, but all the papers will tell you it was Pascal Planche.

You stayed another few minutes on the step before pulling yourself together. It isn't enough never again to set foot in that office. You must also look the doctor in the face to tell him: you're useless and you're fired. This time, all the doors were open. You went right in and saw the man on the floor, the red flood on the blue shirt, the eyes and mouth wide open in one last gasp of incomprehension.

You will not find out what drove Pascal Planche to do this. You will learn only that the doctor's letter opener was found in his apartment, and tests prove

without a doubt that it is the murder weapon. You
will conclude that your own knives—lugged from the
12th to the 10th then on to the 5th arrondissements and
so on—were never involved. Proof: they have been returned to your husband.

Three months after the incident, when you left the
Hôtel-Dieu, you were handed a copy of your medical
file. You studied it, frowning with concentration. You
read and reread it without recognizing anyone in that
pileup of technical terms like the ones in lab reports. You
tried to understand. At your local library, you exam-
ined journals, specialized dictionaries, but all you saw
were white pages streaked with tiny black insects, and
those signs supposedly representing letters that would
then clump into words and sentences and paragraphs
did not trace any intelligible pattern. You observed the
people around you, bent over voluminous works from
which they were gleaning notes meticulously recorded
on index cards. They seemed to understand; to them the
words were meaningful. You would have liked to question them, these students, job hunters, lovers of psychological curiosities. Afraid of revealing terrible secrets,
secrets accessible to everyone save yourself, you didn't
dare say it's for a friend, I'm doing research so I can help

her. Folding and refolding the medical file, you transformed it into a paper boat and you went to the Bassin de la Villette, the largest artificial lake in Paris, where the water had frozen in large sheets drifting beneath the orange sun. You set the boat in the lake, then turned your back on it.

Out on the terrace, you watch the birds circling in the sky until the day vanishes completely beneath the horizon. Then you enter the bedroom where the baby is resting under the coursing lions and galloping giraffes, who settle down at your touch. The child tries out a few *vocalises*, exploring the variations of her instrument a little more methodically, and you reply with distracted enthusiasm. Her warbling grows more elaborate every day. She fuels the dialogue with smiles; she questions, suggests, protests, wriggles like a bug on its back, laughing in the hope of winning you to her side. In the end you take her in your arms to rock her dreamily from side to side, up and down, in more and more of a daze.

PUBLISHING IN THE
PUBLIC INTEREST

Thank you for reading this book published by The New Press. The New Press is a nonprofit, public interest publisher. New Press books and authors play a crucial role in sparking conversations about the key political and social issues of our day.

We hope you enjoyed this book and that you will stay in touch with The New Press. Here are a few ways to stay up to date with our books, events, and the issues we cover:

- Sign up at www.thenewpress.com/subscribe to receive updates on New Press authors and issues and to be notified about local events
- Like us on Facebook: www.facebook.com/newpressbooks
- Follow us on Twitter: www.twitter.com/thenewpress

Please consider buying New Press books for yourself; for friends and family; or to donate to schools, libraries, community centers, prison libraries, and other organizations involved with the issues our authors write about.

The New Press is a 501(c)(3) nonprofit organization. You can also support our work with a tax-deductible gift by visiting www.thenewpress.com/donate.

DECK   CEN
Deck, Julia.
Viviane /

CENTRAL LIBRARY
03/15